My Name is Sahal

A Journey of Exile, Love, and Legacy

Nuur Hassan

Grosvenor House
Publishing Limited

The right of Nuur Hassan to be identified as the author of this
work has been asserted in accordance with Section 78
of the Copyright, Designs and Patents Act 1988

The book cover is copyright to Nuur Hassan

This book is published by
Grosvenor House Publishing Ltd
Link House
140 The Broadway, Tolworth, Surrey, KT6 7HT.
www.grosvenorhousepublishing.co.uk

This book is a work of fiction. Any resemblance to
people or events, past or present, is purely coincidental.

A CIP record for this book
is available from the British Library

Paperback ISBN 978-1-83615-435-8
eBook ISBN 978-1-83615-436-5

Preface

Memory, Loss and Becoming

I began writing *My Name is Sahal* out of a restlessness I could no longer quiet. I belong to the Somali generation born in the early 1970s, a cohort that grew up beneath the broad shade of a peaceful state, only to watch that shade vanish overnight in a devastating civil war. I learned early that when a country collapses, the past becomes slippery unless someone writes it down. Memory came first. I set out to record the rhythms of a childhood, not out of nostalgia but out of duty.

I wanted to preserve the morning bell at Baidoa Primary School, the scent of chalk dust on a warm breeze in Marka during my secondary school years, and the laughter that rang down neighbourhood streets in a country where every auntie was your mother and every elder your teacher.

If memory is the rope that hauls us back from forgetting, then Sahal's voice is my firm attempt to strengthen that rope, tugging readers towards a Somalia many have never seen.

But we cannot speak of memory without speaking of loss. Civil war tore through the country just as my peer group stood at the gate of adulthood. Some of us fled the country; others died in the war, and countless more survived and remained there, shouldering burdens the world seldom notices.

Loss in this novel is not an abstract headline or an academic exercise; it is a father buried in a hurry, a letter that never arrives, a mother separated from her child, a border guard who mispronounces your name and, with it, destroys your very sense of self. I have tried to honour those silences, not to reopen wounds but to acknowledge them. Grief, after all, is evidence that love once lived.

Yet *My Name is Sahal* is ultimately a story of becoming. I wrote it to show that survival is more than endurance; it is evolution. Sahal travels from the dust of Baidoa to the drizzle of Manchester, stumbling, apologising, and rising again. He marries, studies, raises a son, and opens a classroom where other displaced boys and girls learn to code their way into tomorrow.

His journey is imperfect and unfinished, much like our own, but it shows that identity can stretch without tearing and that dignity can flower in unlikely soil. You can be both Somali and British at the same time.

I offer this novel as a lantern, a torch for anyone searching the dark corridors of dislocation, Somali or otherwise. If you recognise your own family's laughter in Sahal's memories, if you feel your own heart tighten at his losses, or if you draw courage from his slow, stubborn becoming, then this book has done what I hoped it would.

To those who never had the chance or the paper to record their stories, this is my small attempt to keep the light alive. May we remember, may we mourn, and, above all, may we continue becoming.

Dedication

To the generation born in Somalia in the 1970s,
tested by war and scattered across continents,
your story lives between these pages.

Acknowledgements

This novel is a tapestry woven from the threads of memory, resilience, and love that define the Somali experience.

My deepest gratitude goes to the generation born in the 1970s in Somalia, whose lives were shaped by peace, tested by war, and carried across continents, inspired this story. Your courage and stories, shared in homes, mosques, and community gatherings, gave Sahal his voice.

I am thankful for the Somali diaspora, in the UK, Europe, US, Canada and Australia, whose vibrancy and strength breathe life into these pages.

To the elders, parents, and teachers who passed down our language, traditions, and faith, your wisdom shaped this narrative, even if your names remain unwritten.

I owe a special debt to the spirit of Baidoa its dusty streets and enduring memories which anchored this journey.

To my readers, especially those who see their own stories reflected in Sahal's, thank you for carrying this lantern forward. Your engagement keeps our history alive.

Finally, to my family, whose love and sacrifices echo in every chapter, this book is as much yours as it is mine.

Contents

Prologue

My name is Sahal

Once, I was a boy growing up in lush Baidoa, in a country full of light and promise. I wanted to become a teacher. I believed in books, blackboards and the slow, beautiful work of building a future. I loved a girl named Hindiyeey, and I thought love, like knowledge, could be built brick by brick, over time and peacefully.

Then everything fell apart.

The war came suddenly, ripping through the streets of Mogadishu, tearing families and futures to pieces. One day, we were students; the next, we were scattered across the earth, as if a tornado had swept us up. I fled with my family to Kenya, then to Europe – alone, carrying only fragments of home, hope and Hindiyeey in my heart.

For years, I worked jobs that no one saw: I silently filled supermarket shelves, I washed cars in the cold rain of Frankfurt, but I never stopped waiting for a letter, a phone call, a whisper that she was still somewhere in the world.

This is a story of exile and return, of a love that crossed borders, and a life rebuilt from the ruins of war. It is the story of Hindiyeey and me: dreams deferred but not destroyed, car washes and classrooms, prayers whispered in cramped rooms, and a baby born into hope. It is a journey across nations, through loss, longing and unexpected grace. And, in the end, it is a story of home, not the one we fled, but the one we chose, built and claimed as ours in a city called Manchester. It is a story of how a name, held firm in the storm, can still carry a soul safely home.

Part I – Beginnings

A Boy With So Much Hair

It was Wednesday, 21 April 1971, just five minutes before midnight, when my mother went into labour. After a remarkably painless delivery lasting only twenty minutes, my maternal grandmother, Nuurto, who had acted as midwife, joyfully exclaimed, 'It's a boy! A dark boy with lots of hair!'

In a state of sheer elation, my Father rushed into the hut to catch a glimpse of me. My mother, relieved but still recovering from her labour, handed me to my Father, who could not conceal his delight at holding his firstborn child. Following tradition, the men then left the dwelling, leaving the female relatives to support the new mother in her recovery. It would be a day before the extended family gathered to bestow a name upon me.

My Father, Diinoow, along with his brother, who was visiting, made their way to the hut where my mother Suleey, my grandmother Nuurto, her sister Sonkoreey, and I – the as-yet-unnamed infant, were sheltering. After exchanging greetings, my Father enquired about my mother's well-being and whether a name had been chosen for me. Before my mother could respond, Sonkoreey proposed 'Kuuloow', meaning 'darkie', as my complexion was significantly darker than my parents. My grandmother Nuurto, however, promptly dismissed this suggestion and hesitated only briefly before suggesting I should be named 'Rooboow', after the rainy season. Suddenly, my mother, who had been awaiting her turn to suggest a name, declared that I should be called 'Gooni', meaning 'solitary one', as I was born on a Wednesday, and local lore claimed that children born on this day tended to be socially awkward and solitary as they grew older.

My Father, a man of few words, at least in public, neither accepted nor rejected any of the proposed names. Then, out of nowhere, my uncle, the semi-literate uncle responsible for recording my date of birth, broke his silence and proclaimed that I should be named 'Sahal', meaning 'easy', as my birth had been effortless and pain-free. One by one, everyone agreed, including my Father.

As the firstborn, I spent my first years primarily surrounded by my mother's family – my grandmother, her sister and my maternal uncle and aunt. During these formative three years, my Father was largely absent from my life. I spent my first two years amidst the goats and sheep, with my Father frequently away from home. One fateful day, a terrifying incident occurred that left my mother shaken. A she-camel, tied up near the hut where my mother and I lived, broke free from her rope and stampeded. In a stroke of misfortune, her kick narrowly missed my mother but struck me instead. Once the camel was eventually brought under control, my mother burst into tears, overwhelmed by the realisation that I had only narrowly escaped death or serious injury. The cries and commotion resulting from the stampede reduced everyone at the scene to tears. Suddenly, a mournful song, lamenting my Father's absence, filled the air, started by my grandmother, Nuurto. 'Sahal, you are here all alone, with only your mother by your side. Your Father has shamelessly deserted you under the cloak of darkness,' she sang, sorrowfully. Sonkoreey, naturally gifted with words, joined in the lament. 'Your Father has vanished, leaving you behind, innocently nursing from your mother's breast. You nearly lost your life because your Father shamelessly vanished under the cover of night.'

Following a suggestion from her family, it was decided that my mother would leave behind the nomadic life, with its constant threat of stampeding animals, and seek a better life for herself and me in Baidoa, the nearest and largest city in the region. My Father, if he so desired, could join us there, as it seemed clear that rural life had become too arduous for him. However, before the plan to relocate to Baidoa could be set in motion, my Father, Diinoow, unexpectedly reappeared.

Upon his unannounced arrival, my mother, though kind-hearted and forgiving, was initially overcome with anger and berated him for abandoning his only son, who was not yet three years old. My Father, accepting full responsibility, expressed his remorse and vowed never to disappear again without a valid reason. My mother, still seething with anger from the incident that had nearly claimed my life and exhausted from my Father's frequent disappearances, summoned him to a pivotal meeting – a make-or-break moment for their relationship. 'Diinoow, we need to talk. I can't go on like this,' she began, her voice raw with frustration. 'You know Sahal is barely three years old, yet you've barely spent three consecutive months with him since he joined us in this life. You're fully aware of what happened the other day when he was almost killed by that stampeding she-camel. Diinoow, I can't continue living like this. I need you to be with us all the time. I need you to be with your son, always.'

My Father, typically a man of few words, was taken aback by my mother's heartfelt ultimatum. He took a moment to collect his thoughts before responding to her plea. Then, all of a sudden, the floodgates opened, and he poured out his feelings. 'Suleey, listen to me carefully. You know I struggle to express myself clearly. I may not show my emotions outwardly, but please believe me when I say that I love you and our firstborn son deeply. I will do whatever it takes to protect both of you. Suleey, I have high ambitions for our son and for you. I dream big for our family, and rural life is not where I see our future, but I don't have the means to move us to Baidoa right now. I am trying to start a business, hoping that it will generate enough profit for us to buy a house in Baidoa or, at the very least, enable us to rent one. I'm begging for your understanding,' my Father pleaded, his voice filled with desperation and hope.

But my mother, unyielding in her resolve, was not swayed by his pleas. She looked directly into his eyes and declared, 'Diinoow, I am moving Sahal and myself to Baidoa, come what may. I am determined to ensure the safety of our son, even if it means risking homelessness. I refuse to live in constant fear of uncontrollable animals that could harm him.' Hearing these words, my Father turned to leave without uttering a word, his head bowed in defeat.

However, after two steps, he abruptly turned back to my mother once more. 'Suleey, I am well aware that your mother Nuurto, and your aunt Sonkoreey have never been my biggest supporters. They disapprove of my constant disappearances, and I understand their concerns. But you are my wife, and we share a son. We have cherished memories, and I implore you not to let their disapproval weigh heavily on our marriage. I have big dreams for both of you,' my Father pleaded, his head still bowed.

He continued, his voice filled with vulnerability and pain, 'I know that Nuurto and Sonkoreey have expressed their grief in a poem lamenting my absence. You know how deeply those words have touched me. It hurts me to hear my mother-in-law's lament. Her poem has reached as far as my own family, and the entire village is aware of its existence. People perceive me as a failure, someone who has failed in the most sacred duty of protecting his family. But I want you to understand, Suleey, that I am not a failure. Despite my absence from the life of our firstborn – and from you – I am not a failure. I am just trying to find my footing, to establish myself on solid ground.' My Father's voice trembled with emotion as he spoke, tears welling in his eyes.

Witnessing his genuine remorse, my mother could not help but feel a trace of empathy for my Father: she recognised the depth of the pain he felt at my grandmother's poignant poem.

However, she remained resolute in her determination not to let her plan be delayed for even a single day. 'Diinoow, I hear you, and I am sorry if my mother's poem has touched you deeply. But you left your son and me alone. All I want is to take our son out of harm's way and move to Baidoa,' she asserted firmly.

The Cute Boy Steps into a
Whole New World!

One cold and sunny morning, my maternal uncle arrived at our hut, driving a blue Range Rover. After briefly exchanging greetings with my mother and the rest of the family, including my Father Diinoow, my uncle asked my mother to prepare for a trip to Baidoa – a one-way journey. While my mother was overjoyed that her older brother was assisting us in travelling to Baidoa and leaving rural life behind, my Father felt a sense of embarrassment because he had wanted to take charge of this trip himself. Yet my mother had to make the arrangements on her own, with the support of her brother, as my Father had still not firmly committed to the move to Baidoa.

After two hours of travelling on rough roads, we arrived in Baidoa – a sprawling urban centre and the largest city in the region. As we made our way through the streets, numerous children ran after the blue Range Rover. My maternal uncle, a sergeant in the Somali National Army, was a generous man who had been in favour of my Mother and Father moving to the city, but only once I was old enough to attend school. However, the incident that had nearly taken my life had changed everyone's perspective, except for my Father, who seemed determined to make the move on his own terms.

'Is that you, Sahal? The cute boy who's stepping into a whole new world?' a voice called out from my right. I turned to see a larger-than-life woman with a wide smile approaching me, her arms outstretched. Unsure of who she was, I was gripped by fear and instinctively ran to my mother's side. My Father quickly reassured me, saying, 'This is Dahaba, a relative of your grandma Nuurto.'

Dahaba, a wealthy yet childless woman and a close relative of my grandmother, invited us to stay in her house until we could afford a place of our own. We lived with her for three months, and she showed us great kindness and hospitality. During this time, my Father, with the assistance of his brother in Mogadishu, managed to purchase a house not far from Dahaba's house. Although it was not as grand as Dahaba's house, it would become my childhood home with so many memories.

From Ukuroow to Adan Dheere

My Father took me to a school outfitters where we encountered a short, fast-talking man named Ukuroow. Every time my Father attempted to ask a question about the school uniform, Ukuroow would cut him off. The shopkeeper greeted us as soon as we entered, exclaiming, 'Good day, new customers! Am I correct in assuming that you need a school uniform for this cute boy?' He looked at me with his small eyes and a wide smile.

My Father responded promptly, 'Yes, that's right. We need a school uniform for him. He's starting school in two weeks.' However, before my Father could finish his sentence, Ukuroow enthusiastically pointed to some shirts and trousers, exclaiming, 'Yes, yes, we have them! Cute boy, you're going to school next week!' His small eyes sparkled as he spoke.

My Father proceeded to inspect the various trousers and shirts available, eventually selecting an appropriate school uniform for me. As he prepared to pay, Ukuroow interjected once again, his words flying out rapidly, 'Am I correct to assume that he also needs school shoes?' My Father, slightly exhausted by Ukuroow's rapid speech, replied, 'No, he already has school shoes.' My Father knew that I had no school shoes, but he intended to find and purchase them from another shop. With a final farewell, 'Bye, cute boy! Be good at school!' Ukuroow's eyes almost disappeared behind his smile, which remained as wide as ever. I looked at him silently, gripping my Father's hand as tightly as I could as we stepped out of his shop.

Two more weeks passed until the official start of the school year for six-year-olds like me. However, three days before my first day, my Father informed my mother that he would be away as he needed to close a business deal in a nearby village. Although my mother was not pleased that he would not be there on such an important day, she was less angry than she had been during my Father's previous disappearances. After all, at least she would not have to worry about stampeding animals this time.

Finally, the big day arrived. My mother prepared my breakfast and woke me up earlier than usual, filled with excitement. 'Sahal, wake up, Hooyo! It's your first day of school,' she called. I leapt out of bed with enthusiasm, responding, 'Haye, Hooyo', a mixture of hope and fear filling my voice as I pondered what the day had in store for me.

The primary school was not far from our home, just a ten-minute walk at most. Upon our arrival, we were greeted by the school's principal, Aliyoow – a short, stocky man with a bald head and a bushy moustache that hovered over a gap in his teeth. His voice, deep and somewhat intimidating, boomed from behind his moustache as he greeted me, 'Good morning, young man.' Before I could reply, Aliyoow pointed towards his office and said in an equally commanding voice, 'Before you join your class, we have some paperwork to complete. Let's go to my office.'

My mother, a slightly built and smaller-than-average woman, was nevertheless taller than Aliyoow. That is how short the principal was, but what he lacked in height, he made up for with his booming voice and intimidating presence.

Aliyoow opened a red file and turned his attention to my mother, saying, 'I will need your son's full name, date of birth, and the names of his parents.' My mother promptly provided all the requested information. It felt as though hours passed as we completed the paperwork, and I could not shake off the feeling that I was about to be separated from my mother forever.

Finally, Aliyoow stood up abruptly and announced, 'He is now ready to join his class.' I looked at my mother, a sense of trepidation washing over me. I clutched my backpack tightly and followed Aliyoow after bidding my mother goodbye.

I entered a noisy but surprisingly well-behaved classroom where somewhat apprehensive pupils sat in rows. I took a seat next to Hassanoow, who would later become a childhood friend. About ten minutes after I had entered the class, a teacher arrived with a red book, chalk, and a stick in hand. The entire class fell silent, as if every child feared the stick.

'Good morning, pupils,' the teacher intoned in a soft but authoritative voice.

'Good morning, teacher,' the class responded in unison.

The teacher introduced himself, saying, 'My name is Macalin Adan Dheere and I'll be teaching you the alphabet. You will learn how to read and write this year. You will need to pay attention. Do you understand?'

Thinking that the other pupils would respond in unison, I enthusiastically replied, 'Haa Macalin', much to the surprise of both the teacher and my fellow pupils. As I sat there, the entire class turned to look at me, their eyes fixed on me in astonishment. Feeling a little scared, I looked down, avoiding their intense gaze.

However, to my surprise, the teacher walked over to me and asked, 'What is your name, young man?' I replied, 'Sahal', rather more hesitantly than before. He replied, 'Nice to meet you, Sahal. You are a very confident young boy. Well done.'

The day came to an end, and I felt emotionally drained, from the first encounter with the intimidating principal to the classroom where I had unintentionally attracted more attention than I had planned.

Macalin Adan Dheere was my class's only teacher for the entire year and always emphasised the importance of discipline and punctuality. Aware of my teacher's strict approach, my mother adopted a routine of waking me up early, preparing my breakfast and ensuring my school clothes were ready. As a result, I would leave home earlier than most of my friends, arriving at school well before the gates opened.

Unexpectedly, my friend Hassanoow adopted a similar routine, which allowed us to spend more time together before the official start of the school day. We would chat, play and engage in various activities. One of our favourite pastimes was exploring the area around the termite mountain near the school, playing games like hide and seek.

These early-morning adventures not only strengthened our friendship but also provided a sense of joy and camaraderie before the structured school day began. Little did we know that these moments would later become such cherished memories.

Grief, Growth and Longing for a Father

In the Shadow of Grief, I Longed Not Just for a Teacher, but for a Father.

In my second year, Macalin Adan Dheere fell ill and unfortunately never returned to teaching. In his place, we were introduced to a new teacher named Saneey. Unlike his predecessor, Saneey was known for his fast-paced talk and stern expression. However, behind that stern facade, he proved to be very helpful and less strict than our previous teacher.

With the arrival of Saneey, our curriculum expanded to include subjects such as mathematics, history, science and geography. It was a significant step forward in our educational journey. Saneey was particularly animated when teaching history: he would passionately share stories of wars, showcase images of historical figures and delve into the intricacies of past events. Despite his initially intimidating demeanour, his enthusiasm for history ignited a newfound interest in the subject among many students: we found ourselves eagerly absorbing the lessons, captivated by his engaging teaching style.

One day, in the middle of class, the school principal, Aliyoow, suddenly appeared in our classroom. 'Saneey, can I have a word?' he asked, his commanding tone tinged with sadness. Instantly, the atmosphere in the classroom shifted, and a sense of unease washed over us. We knew that something significant had happened, as the principal never interrupted classes unless it was urgent.

Saneey stepped outside to speak with the principal, leaving the rest of us waiting in silence. After what felt like an eternity, he returned to the classroom, his expression sombre and his eyes downcast, on the verge of tears. Jamiilo, who was usually quiet and reserved, broke the silence, her voice unnaturally loud, 'Macalin maxaa dhacay? What happened, teacher?'

Saneey did not respond immediately, leaving the entire class on edge. Eventually, he cleared his throat and addressed us, 'Class, I have something to tell you.' The room fell into complete silence as all eyes turned to him, awaiting his words anxiously. He hesitated for a moment before delivering the heartbreaking news, 'It is with great sadness that I have to report to you that Macalin Adan Dheere passed away peacefully last night, surrounded by his family.'

As soon as the words left his lips, tears welled up in Saneey's eyes, breaking through his usually calm and composed demeanour. Most of us were between the ages of 7 and 8, and we struggled to comprehend the gravity of the news. Macalin Adan Dheere had been our beloved teacher in our first year of school, guiding us through the early stages of our education. He was more than just a teacher to us – he had been a Father figure, a role model and a source of comfort.

The realisation that we would never see him again hit us like a wave of grief. Jamiilo suddenly burst into tears, triggering a collective wailing throughout the classroom, as each of us grappled with the loss in our own way. 'Ow our macalin, ow our macalin, does that mean we will never see Macalin Adan Dheere ever again?' echoed through the room, with mingled sorrow and disbelief.

The impromptu wailing continued for what felt like an eternity until, eventually, the classroom fell silent once more. Saneey tried to offer words of comfort, but the wailing started again, 'Ow our macalin, ow our macalin.' Saneey, now overcome with tears himself, summoned the strength to speak in a loud, trembling voice. 'Class, I hear your sorrow, I hear you, please,' he began, his voice quivering with emotion.

'Macalin Adan Dheere is gone; may Allah have mercy on his soul. No, we will never see him again, but his memory will live on with us.'

He paused, taking a moment to compose himself before continuing. 'You may not know this, but Macalin Adan Dheere was a childhood friend of mine. He was my classmate and we went to school together. He was a good man, a great friend and like a brother to me.' This revelation brought a new depth to our understanding of the loss we were experiencing. Saneey's connection to our former teacher added a layer of poignancy to the situation, emphasising the profound impact that Macalin Adan Dheere had on those around him.

We finished lessons early, in grief. Despite Saneey's attempts, intermittent outbursts of wailing continued, repeating the same sentences, 'Ow our macalin, ow our macalin. Does that mean we will never see Macalin Adan Dheere ever again?' On the way home, Hassanoow and I walked silently, not saying a word, but inwardly replaying again and again the same wailing uttered in the class, 'Ow our macalin, ow our macalin. Does that mean we will never see Macalin Adan Dheere again?'

I reached home earlier than usual from school, and my mother wanted to know why. 'Sahal, is everything alright? You are early today?'

Without hesitation, I said, 'Yes, mum, I am early today because we finished early.'

My mother was taken aback by my vehement response and said, 'Why, what happened. You don't seem right, Hooyo?' Out of nowhere, I let out a high-pitched cry.

'Macalin Adan Dheere has passed away peacefully, surrounded by his family,' I cried, repeating verbatim Saneey's words when he broke the news, adding only, 'and we will never see him again.'

My mother was frozen with shock; not knowing how to process the news, she simply stood in silence. After a few moments, she said, 'May Allah have mercy on his soul and give patience to his family.' She then sat me down, took off my school bag and helped me change out of my uniform.

The following day, the school principal, Aliyoow, came with his deputy to talk to the class and address our grief, because Macalin Adan Dheere had been our only teacher throughout the previous year, so if any class needed counselling, it would be ours. Aliyoow and his deputy, with our teacher Saneey beside them, talked to us at length and told us that while the news was tragic, we needed to move on and make our late teacher proud by excelling in our schoolwork. We finished the year on a shaky note and seemed not to have recovered from the loss of our first teacher.

During the later part of the year, my Father was away for most of the time, only at home for a few weeks at a time. However, he kept sending money and long letters to my mother. My Father was illiterate, as was my mother, but he managed to get his business partner, a man whose name he would never reveal, to write letters from dictation. My mother would ask me to read my Father's letters to her, and sometimes, when I struggled to read perfectly, she would ask Aunt Dahaba from next door, the woman with whom we stayed before we had our own house. Aunt Dahaba had dropped out of school, but due to her passion for literature, she became a highly literate woman who read widely in Somali and Italian. Indeed, she spoke fluent Italian, like her late Father, who had been a bureaucrat in the Italian colonial administration. My Father initially sent letters just to my mother; later, he would from time to time send two letters: one for her and one for me.

Letters addressed to my mother would always start with the words, 'Dear sweetheart Suleey, it is me, your loving but absent husband, Diinoow.' He would go on to talk about the state of his business, how he was turning a corner and expected to make us all rich in no time, but how she needed to be patient with his extended absence. He would end by saying how proud he was of her continued love and the support she gave him.

Year 2 at school ended well for me. I gained some of the best grades for all my subjects, but the extended absence of my Father was starting to affect me psychologically: I wanted my Father to attend parents' meetings with me, not just my mother all the time. I saw my classmates all coming in with their fathers, while my Father was absent. When the end-of-term reports were distributed, all parents whose children had received top grades were invited by the principal to an event celebrating their children's achievements. My mother and I went along with all the other parents and their children. Only two students from my year group, including me, had achieved the top grade across all subjects, so the evening was quite nerve-wracking for me on two accounts: firstly, I only knew one student out of the twenty attending the event and, secondly, while the other children had their mothers and fathers with them, I only had my mother, who could not read or write. My turn came; I was called to the podium and, feeling uncomfortable, I went up to receive a certificate of excellence from the principal and from my teacher, Saneey, followed by a few words of congratulations from the principal, Aliyoow.

'Sahal was the shyest pupil when I first met him in my office on the day he started school. Now here he is excelling in all subjects! Very well done, Sahal. Of course,' he continued, 'we must also acknowledge his parents, without whom he would not have achieved such grades. Where are your Mother and Father, Sahal?' I pointed towards the audience and said, 'That's my mother, but my Father is not here.' Aliyoow immediately responded in his usual loud and intimidating voice, 'Oh, so that is your mother, but your Father is not here.' Although I was ecstatic about my achievement and the compliments I got from my teacher and the principal, the words 'But your Father is not here' fell me. I felt empty: I wanted my Father to be with me and I wanted to be like the other children whose parents were both present. I could see the disappointment in my mother's face as she looked down on hearing these words, but my mother is one of those women who rarely show their emotions, least of all in front of their children. When she saw that I was looking at her, she forced herself to smile. After we came home from the event, however, the words hit her harder, and I heard her say under her breath, 'Diinoow, he can't even be with his son in a moment of celebration.' As soon as she realised that I had heard this, she tried to change the subject as if it had not happened. Weeks passed, and my mother still had traces of disappointment on her face. Most evenings, except Fridays, Aunt Dahaba would stop to say hello and, without fail, bring halwa and home-made cake. I loved eating Aunt Dahaba's halwa so much that I got sick one day after eating such a big portion that I had to be taken to hospital, but after a few days of skipping it, I went back to eating it every week.

Aunt Dahaba would, without fail, ask me about my school work and whether I had good friends, and then, before she left, would ask my mother about my Father, 'Ninkii diinoow ahaa wali ma maqanyahay?' 'Is Diinoow still away?', and my mother would say, 'Haa wali wuu ma qanyahay. Yes, he is still away,' with an undertone of shame. However, that evening, before Aunt Dahaba waved us goodbye, my mother requested her help in composing a letter to my Father.

As I sat next to her, my mother started dictating to Aunt Dahaba, her voice going up and down, emphasising some words more than others.

Dear Husband,

After warm greetings, I am writing this letter as usual with the help of Aunt Dahaba; what is unusual about this letter, though, is that your son, Sahal, is sitting right next to me, and he can hear all my dictation. Diinoow, it has been six months since you were last home. As you know, six months is a long time for your son, who is only eight years old. He has just finished his second year at school and is constantly scanning the room to find a Father figure, a male figure that he can learn from, a male figure that he can play football with but, sadly, you are not there for him, nor do I have a relative to fill your shoes. This, as you are perfectly well aware, is affecting his sense of who he is, his sense of belonging. Before you went on this trip six months ago, you promised to return home in time for your son's end-of-year presentation at school and to at least attend it with me so that we could show him how much we love him. Sadly, like other promises in the past, you have not honoured this one either. I am saddened on two fronts. First, you have missed your son's celebration of being one of the top of his class across all subjects. This achievement would make any parent proud of their child, but Sahal had to be content with his Father being absent and only having the company of his mother, who is tired of being on her own. Secondly, your absence is no longer simply a family issue but has now been noticed by the leaders of our son's school. I will not repeat what was said after the principal found out that you were absent, and it was only me there when all the other children had both their fathers and mothers there. Diinoow, I need you back home, and your son needs you back home; your extended absence is affecting both of us negatively. In your last letter, you promised us you would be home in three months, but it is now six months. From here on, I should stop counting the months or believing your promises. Diinoow, I repeat, I need you back home.

Best wishes

Suleey

Before the letter was folded and put in an envelope, we heard a knock on the front door, which was made of corrugated iron. My mother went to investigate, and there was a man there with a letter and money from my Father.

'Are you Suleey?' he asked in a dialect that was not locally spoken.

'Yes, I am Suleey, who are you?' asked my mother in her Maay-Maay dialect. The man appeared to understand but carried on in his Af-Mahaa-tiri dialect.

'I have a letter and money from your husband, Diinoow. I will be in town for a few more days before I go back. If you want to send a letter to your husband, I am happy to take it to him because I will see him on my return.' Aunt Dahaba, the newly written letter in one hand and a brown envelope in the other, and I were now listening attentively to the conversation between my mother and this man.

Then, suddenly, my mother said, still in her Maay-Maay dialect, 'Yes, please, we have a letter and a gift to send to him. Please come back a day before you go, or tell us where you are staying and we will bring it to you.'

'No problem, I will come back the day before I depart, no need for you to come to me,' said the man in his Af-Mahaa-tiri dialect.

'Thank you,' said my mother, waving to the man and closing the corrugated iron door behind him.

As soon as she closed the door, she saw Aunt Dahaba and me standing behind her; although we pretended not to have heard the conversation between them, she easily guessed that we had. 'Who was the man with the Af-Mahaa-tiri dialect?' asked Aunt Dahaba.

My mother started to explain, but my aunt interrupted, laughing, 'We heard all the conversation! Do you want me to read the letter for you before I go home?'

'Yes, please, you know I can't read, and Sahal is not a fluent reader yet.'

My mother handed the envelope to Aunt Dahaba, who opened it hastily. 'A two-page letter!' she exclaimed.

'Dear sweetheart Suleey, It is me, your loving but absent husband, Diinoow.

I pray that this letter reaches you and Sahal' – normally, my Father would refer to me as his son, not by my first name, but in this letter, he calls me by my name. Aunt Dahaba eagerly continued to read the letter. 'I want to tell you that my persistence in making our dream of financial security a reality is yielding dividends. My business partner and I have now got a new product in our shops that no other business is selling. This product line is from Kenya, and we are getting it duty-free to our shops. My love, money will soon be the least worry for you and our son – you will live a life of comfort, but before that, I need you to continue to exercise patience. My love, this may not be what you wanted to hear, but this type of business takes longer than others and needs my full attention, hence my extended absence from your life and the life of my son. Raage, who delivered this letter and some money for the next two months, will have told you how hard I work...' When my Aunt Dahaba read the words, 'Next two months,' she stopped and looked at my mother as if to say, Diinoow will be away another two months. Without saying a word, Aunt Dahaba's eyes moved back to the letter and started reading again. 'My love, I have a grand plan to make us all financially secure in a short period of time, so please continue to exercise patience with my extended absence. The money I sent you will be sufficient to cover your and Sahal's living expenses for two months or slightly more. However, that doesn't mean that I will not come home before the end of two months.' Suddenly, Aunt Dahaba stopped reading and, like earlier, looked at my mother as if to say, 'Diinoow may show up sooner.' With a smile, she went back to reading the letter, but it ended abruptly one sentence later, 'I love you and my son, and I can't wait to see you both soon.'

Aunt Dahaba folded the letter, put it back in its original envelope and handed the letter to my mother. My mother looked exhausted and did not know what to make of it, whether to be happy or unhappy, whether to believe it or not, whether to tear it up or keep to re-read. I was going through similar turmoil, but mine was filled with anger at my Father, firstly because he had not mentioned my schoolwork or how I was doing, or the celebration for my academic achievement. Of course, in the case of the last, my anger was misplaced, as my Father could not have known about an event that took place only a week before. Secondly, I was angry that my Father was prioritising business success over his family and paying no attention to the effect that his extended absence was having on my emotional well-being. Aunt Dahaba left to go home as it was getting late for her dinner. After she had gone, my mother and I spent a good part of the evening not saying anything to one another – all the stranger because my mother has always a story or two to tell and is never on her own while I am at home. Dinner came later than usual and while we were eating, my mother said in her usual reassuring tones, 'Your Father will soon be coming home. He is working hard to make us financially secure.' On one hand, this was reassuring, and I was happy to hear it, but on the other, I was confused because my mother was repeating my Father's words when she appeared not to believe them.

Exactly two months later, my Father arrived unexpectedly in the middle of the night. I was asleep when he arrived, and I only realised he was there in the morning when I woke up for school. 'Sahal, my boy, how are you?' asked my Father loudly, shocked that I was not expecting him.

I replied, 'I am good.'

He continued in the same loud voice, 'You are a big boy now, no words can capture how proud I am to see you grow up that fast ... and your mother has told me all about your school achievements and how you were given a certificate for achieving the top grades across all your subjects ... no words can capture how proud I am of you,' he continued without a pause. 'I came home in the small hours and you were fast asleep, so I did not want to disturb you, knowing it is a school day for you.' Meeting my Father after eight months brought mixed emotions; on one hand, I was delighted to see a Father whom I had missed sorely. On the other hand, I was still angry about him being away for so long.

'Get ready for school, son, I will take you to the shops and buy you whatever you want,' said my Father with a big smile. Before I could say anything, my mother, who was preparing breakfast in the kitchen, shouted, 'Anything?' and my Father looked at me and said, 'Yes, anything,' with a smile. That day, I went to school feeling energised and told my friend Hassanoow that my Father was back in town and that I was going shopping with him after school, as if to say, 'I have a Father too.' But inside, I knew that Hassanoow's Father was the opposite of mine: he was always at home, never missed a parent meeting at school, and never appeared to have the grand ambitions my Father talked about. Part of me wanted my Father to be like Hassanoow's, and part of me loved my Father as he was. Three weeks later, my Father went back to his business, which was now permanently located in a small town on the border of Kenya and Somalia. Those three weeks were the longest I can remember my Father being at home. I really enjoyed them: every day after school, my Father would take me to the city centre and buy me an ice cream, and then we would walk back home. While I thoroughly enjoyed my Father's company, I knew it would not last and that one day he would have to go back to his business.

When my Father went back, my mother did not seem as sad as in previous years, but the struggle of being alone, with her husband constantly away on business trips, was written clearly on her face, even if she tried not to show it.

Grandmother's Shadow

My Mother Left to Say Goodbye —
but Who Would Look After Me?

Three months after my Father left on that quiet Friday afternoon, the news came that my maternal grandmother, Nuurto, was very ill and might not survive her illness. It was the first time I had seen my mother cry. My mother and grandmother were very close, and the bond between the two never weakened; even when we moved to Baidoa and she remained in Daynuunaay, she visited us every few months.

My mother was very disturbed by the news. While we were eating breakfast in the kitchen, Aunt Dahaba came by, perhaps to offer her usual morning greetings, which she never misses, or perhaps to console my mother about the serious illness of her mother. Aunt Dahaba was a close relative of my grandmother, and they had always gotten on well. It was Friday, and there was no school. After I finished breakfast, I asked my mother if I could play with Hassanoow, who was waiting outside with a ball in his hand. Hassannow and I were keen football players, and both had pictures of Pele in his famous Brazilian yellow jersey. When I came home, I found Aunt Dahaba still chatting with my mother. I greeted them both and went to get a drink of water. Before I could have a shower, my mother called, in her Bakool Maay-Maay dialect, 'Sahal, can you come here? Aunt Dahaba and I want to talk to you.' I instantly knew something was wrong, as my mother often resorts to her regional dialect when she is in a serious mood or has something important to say. I went over to them and sat down.

After a few moments, Aunt Dahaba broke the silence, 'Sahal, there is something we need to tell you. You have heard by now that your beloved grandmother, the woman who gave birth to your mother, my cousin, and the person who delivered you, is seriously ill.' I suddenly looked at my mother and saw her head bowed and her shoulders collapsed forward. Aunt Dahaba continued in her usual soft Bay Maay-Maay dialect, 'Your Father is not here to take the pressure off your mother's shoulders in this difficult hour, and that is why I am here to help her.' I looked at my mother again: she was still in the same position, except that her shoulders were back in their right place. 'Your mum is travelling tomorrow to Daynuunaay to be at the side of your grandmother. We don't know how long she will be away; everything depends on the illness of your grandmother,' said Aunt Dahaba. Confused, not knowing what she was going to say next, I started breathing heavily and feeling numbness in my legs. I was worried about what would happen to me: my mother was going away, and my Father was already away. Who was going to look after me, and what about my school and the friends I had made there? Was I being completely forgotten? Was I non-existent? These questions raced around my head. I wanted answers, and I wanted them now from my mother and Aunt Dahaba. 'Now, we've decided that you will move into my house – I will look after you until your mother comes back,' said Aunt Dahaba.

My mother took over, 'Hooyo, this is not an easy decision, and I don't want you to feel that you have been left on your own. You know how much I love you, but your beloved grandmother, Nuurto, my mother, and the one who delivered you on a dark and rainy night in Daynuunaay, is very ill. I am not sure if I will get to her in time, that is how serious her illness is.' Tears ran down her cheeks as she continued, 'We hope that as soon as your Father hears the news, he will make his way to you and look after you, but in the meantime, you can stay here with Aunt Dahaba. Of course, I could easily take you to Daynuunaay and you could stay with me while I am looking after your grandmother, but Daynuunaay has no good schools and you are doing so well in school that I don't want to interrupt your education Hooyo.' Tears continued to stream down her cheeks. 'Aunt Dahaba's house is a good house; you are familiar with it as we lived there for three months before we moved into our house, and you know it is not far from the school.' I suddenly looked at Aunt Dahaba, perhaps subconsciously seeking reassurance from her that all would be fine in her home. She nodded and smiled at me as if to say there was nothing to worry about.

Early on the following morning, as planned, a minibus arrived to transport my mother to Daynuunaay. As it was a school day, I went to school knowing that I would neither go back home nor see my mother after school for some time. I had trouble concentrating in lessons, and this was picked up by my teacher, Saneey. 'Sahal, why do you look anxious and restless today?' he asked in front of the class. I did not want to say what had happened, that my Mother had gone to visit my dying grandmother and that I had no one to look after me except my childless and ageing Aunt Dahaba. As the school day ended, I felt exhausted and anxious about going to Aunt Dahaba's house. I refused to play with Hassanoow on my way back home, but Hassanoow knew the situation, so he understood.

I arrived at Aunt Dahaba's house and found her usual bubbly self. 'Here is my son, Sahal, welcome home, Sahal,' she said. Before I could respond, she continued, 'How was school today?'

'Thank you, Aunt Dahaba, school was good,' I replied, not being honest about the day's experience, but I was hot and bothered and wanted to eat and drink, so I decided to leave, telling her, perhaps for another day. After a few days of staying with Aunt Dahaba, however, it all seemed normal: my happiness returned, and I went back to playing with Hassanoow before and after school. From time to time, this returned normality was punctuated by the absence of my Mother.

A few weeks later, we still had no news about my grandmother's condition or my mother's return date, but my Father arrived in Baidoa, perhaps having heard that I was staying with Aunt Dahaba and my mother was in Daynuunaay with her sick mother. Initially, he wanted to take me back to our house and stay with me, but Aunt Dahaba suggested that it would be better for me to continue to stay with her and for my Father to join my mother to support her in this difficult hour. My Father accepted the suggestion without hesitation and left the next day for Daynuunaay.

Exactly one month after my Father joined my mother at the side of my dying grandmother, Nuurto breathed her last. Three days after her funeral, my mother, Father, and Great-Aunt Sonkoreey came back to Baidoa. Since her older sister was no longer there, it was decided that Sonkoreey would stay with us, and my mother would look after her.

My Father came back from Daynuunaay a changed man: he no longer harboured a burning ambition to make money, do well in commerce, or seek social prominence. Something had profoundly changed him; perhaps the death of his mother-in-law had brought him closer to home, perhaps he had thought to himself that life is after all short, and rather than spending months away from his wife and his only son pursuing business riches, he should prioritise his family. Conversely, my mother came back surprisingly strong and accepting of the death of her beloved mother, Nuurto.

After consulting with my mother, my Father sold his business shares to his business partner. He decided to save half the money and gave the other half to my mother, who decided to set up a small corner shop selling household goods in our neighbourhood.

Meeting Hindiyeey

The First Time I Heard Her Name,
I Never Imagined How Much It Would Mean to Me.

After my Father abandoned his business ambitions, we became a happy family and no longer felt abandoned. I continued to do well at school; my Father and mother, like Hassanoow's parents, accompanied me to every parents' evening, and this meant the world to me and to my mother, who had shouldered this duty alone more than she should have had to. There were no more sarcastic comments from the principal or the teachers about my Father's absence because I now had two parents in my life. At school, I became a little arrogant and got into trouble once or twice, once even almost being excluded from school. My Father was aware of this and was not happy about my new behaviour. In consultation with my mother, he decided to move me to another school. Surprisingly, although I missed my friend Hassanoow, I settled in instantly at the new school. It was run by a principal who spoke in the Af-Mahaa Tiri dialect, who was extremely calm but had the reputation of excluding students from school should anyone cross the line. In my new class, there were two star students – Hindiyeey and Siidoow. Hindiyeey was pretty and very bright. We soon became friends, since we both loved maths, and I matched her academic performance. Our friendship solidified in my first week of the new school, when my class was having a mathematics quiz and we were divided into two groups.

Hindiyeey and I were in one group while the other was led by Siidoow. We won the competition very easily, and I answered all my questions correctly. From that day, Hindiyeey became my close friend. Siidoow, however, was anything but friendly; he was territorial and felt threatened by this new rival, competing for the position of top-performing male student, or perhaps he was jealous of my friendship with Hindiyeey, who was now not talking to him as much.

The new school was more affluent than my old one, so I was much tougher and rougher than Siidoow, who did not want to get into a fight with me but was determined to engage in a cold war, in which he competed with me both academically and for the attention of the teachers and Hindiyeey. I held my ground and outperformed him in almost all subjects. My relationship with Hindiyeey blossomed to the extent that, after school, she always invited me to her home – a household much wealthier than mine – and her parents and younger brother Kuusoow seemed to like me too. I finished the year at the top of the class; Hindiyeey was second and Siidoow third by some distance. Despite my close friendship with Hindiyeey, I still kept up my friendship with Hassanoow: we met for football, went to swim together in Garbida and Eel Mukhtari, and competed as to who could do more chin-ups at the Dadabta.

After I completed middle school, my parents concluded that I had some academic talent, and my Father therefore suggested that I should be sent to a boarding school hundreds of miles away in Marka. Although she was initially unhappy with my Father's decision to send me to boarding school at the tender age of fifteen, my mother had no other option but to go along with his decision. Perhaps she was partly persuaded by my enthusiasm and willingness to attend school away from home.

The school was a government-run school, as all schools were then, because at that time, the education system in Somalia was publicly funded from primary to university.

Although there was a small registration fee to enrol each year, this was something that my Father could pay without going into debt or needing to ask for help from anyone else. Furthermore, my mother's corner shop was doing so well that she was contemplating expanding the business by opening another shop in the neighbourhood and hiring a shopkeeper to run it separately. When I started at the new school, I was hit by both a terrible homesickness and the high standards and highly competitive environment. The majority of the students were from either middle-class or upper-middle-class families and had had private tuition throughout primary and middle school in maths, English, and science. Although mathematics and science came naturally to me and I had a great aptitude for numeracy, my family did not have the financial means to pay for a private tutor to teach me English, geography, or history, so I had to compete with highly tutored students. As I found out at the end of year, this was next to impossible: I ended up achieving average grades in mathematics and science and below average in English. The disappointment of my Year 9 under-performance was coupled with the fact that I was away from home and my parents. Every academic term, my Father would send me pocket money. At school, we were given three meals, but most students relied on money sent by their parents to buy extra food and other necessities. The money I was receiving from my Father was not enough; despite my frugality, I always ran out in the middle of the term and would write to my Father begging for more, which I always got, however unsustainable this was for him. I would write,

Dear Aabo,

Hope you and Hooyo are doing well. I am doing well here at school and, as always, I am studying hard to get good grades. Aabo, life here is very expensive and unfortunately, the money you sent me has long run out. Even when I followed Hooyo's

suggestion, which was to go and buy food in the cheapest area of the city, I still keep running out of money. Can you please, Aabo, either increase my termly allowance or send me more money to survive until next term's allowance arrives?

Thank you, Aabo

Sahal

Each time, my Father would immediately send me extra money to last me until the next instalment of my allowance was due. However, one day, my Father appeared unexpectedly at school. Normally, students were not allowed to receive visitors during the school day. However, it was Thursday, the last day of the week before the weekend, so my Father was allowed to visit the campus, and it was a pleasant surprise to see him. After I had shown him around, my Father gave me some money and told me that he wanted me to meet two people in town, so I needed to meet him in the town's livestock market on Friday morning. He did not tell me who these two people were or why we were meeting them, and I did not know that we had any relatives in Marka.

On the following day, I went to town, excited to see my Father again and curious about these two unknown people. I met my Father in a very busy market where people were buying and selling livestock – a trade my Father always liked. We left the market and went to one of the best restaurants in Marka, known as the 'river restaurant'. I had always wanted to go there but had never had enough money to do so. Now that my Father was in town, it seemed perfectly affordable to have breakfast in the restaurant. After the waiter had ushered us to an empty table in the corner, a tall, extremely skinny man with a small bald head came in, greeting my Father loudly.

'Diinoow, the son of my dear aunt Halima, how lovely to see you,' he bellowed, attracting the attention of other people having breakfast.

My Father's response was slightly more muted: 'Hudle, my brother, how lovely to see you, too.' They embraced each other as if they never wanted to let each other go. I sat there, fixated on both of them but mainly looking at Hudle, the unknown relative in Marka. After a few minutes, they sat down at the table, and I became the centre of attention.

'Is this your son, Sahal?' asked Hudle loudly. Hudle's frame was skinny and conspicuously frail, but his voice was anything but; when he spoke, it was as if he had an extra engine on his throat.

'Yes, he is my son, and he is attending Hiloowle boarding school,' responded my Father.

'Oh, Hiloowle boarding school? Since when has he been there?' Hudle asked.

'Only a year, it is early days,' replied my Father. 'Listen, Hudle, the reason I wanted to meet you is that I want you to keep an eye on Sahal. He is a well-balanced boy, but barely 16 years of age, and new to Markan culture and people. Also, I want you to give him anything he needs; I will pay you back when I am in town,' said my Father.

Without hesitating, Hudle – now Uncle Hudle – replied with a big smile. 'Of course, I will look after him and he can come to my shop and get whatever he desires, as long as his Father is going to pay me back.' I realised that Uncle Hudle was missing the entire row of his lower teeth, although I did not know what had happened to him.

'Good, good, thank you, Hudle, I appreciate that. Now, let us order breakfast,' said my Father. They ate camel meat and bread, and I ate a pancake with honeycomb.

'Delicious,' said Hudle, after he had emptied his plate. Uncle Hudle wanted to pay the bill, but my Father vehemently insisted that he had invited Hudle and the breakfast was his treat. Before he left, Uncle Hudle invited me to come and see his shop on the next Friday I was in town, and I accepted his invitation.

My Father and I spent another hour in the restaurant talking about schoolwork and how proud he was of my attitude to learning. All of a sudden, he remembered something.

'Oh no, we have another appointment which I completely forgot.'

'Appointment?' I asked.

'Yes, your mother and I have arranged for Luuleey to give you breakfast every Friday and Saturday when you have no classes.'

'Luuleey? Who's she?' I asked, slightly confused.

'Don't you remember the distant cousin of your mother who used to visit us in Baidoa?'

'No,' was my quick response.

'Okay, well, you will meet her shortly,' my Father said, with a smile on his face.

Luuleey was a childless widow whose husband had died in the Ogaden war of 1977. He had been a much-respected sergeant in the Somali National Army. Luuleey had never remarried after the death of her husband and, in order to make ends meet, was running a breakfast club for students and low-paid civil servants. Her breakfast club was always busy, and the menu was always the same – a pancake with honey and sesame oil on top, and very sweet tea – a choice of white or black. Most of the diners had black tea, but I preferred my tea white, with goats' milk.

When we arrived at Luuleey's breakfast club, it was nearly noon, and she was about to close, already cleaning and mopping the floor. 'Luuleey, how lovely to see you, my sister,' said my Father in a high-pitched voice. Luuleey turned around instantly, aware of our arrival.

'Diinoow, son of my uncle Booroow, how lovely to see you,' she responded. My Father, a devout Muslim, never shook hands with women other than his wife and sisters. Luuleey understood this and placed her hand on her chest – a gesture indicating a handshake. Despite her advancing age and the fact that she lived and worked alone without a husband, Luuleey looked remarkably fit for her age; she was tall, slim, very light-skinned, and well-dressed. Unlike Uncle Hudle, she had heard of me and knew my name. 'Sahal Habaryar iyo Eedo, how is school, and I hope you are happy in Marka?' she said.

Slightly taken aback by her up-to-date knowledge of my situation, I nodded, 'School is good and, erm, Marka is good too.' Luuleey offered us sweet tea with goat's milk, and we spent another hour in her breakfast club.

My Father, following the plan he had already made, said abruptly, 'Luuleey, I would like Sahal to have his breakfast here every Friday and Saturday, when he doesn't have classes. Here is the money for this month,' and he handed over a wad of money to Luuleey. She initially refused to take it, but my Father insisted on leaving the money on her lap.

We left Luuleey's breakfast club and, before I went back to school, my Father suggested that we have lunch together at the river restaurant. It was packed with customers, with orders from diners flying from all directions. As we sat down, the same waiter who had served us in the morning came over to us, 'Can I take your order, please?'

'Yes, I will have brown rice and camel meat; can you make sure the meat is well done?' said my Father.

'I think we have run out of brown rice, but I will ask the chef,' replied the waiter. 'What can I get you, young man?' he asked, looking at his notepad with a pen ready to jot down my order.

'I will have pasta and goat meat, please,' was my response.

'An excellent choice,' said the waiter.

While we were waiting for our orders, my Father, sipping a freshly squeezed mango juice, said, 'Aabo Sahal, I am leaving Marka tomorrow morning for Baidoa. I will go via Mogadishu to say hello to your uncle, who has not been enjoying good health lately. I want you to work hard. Aabo, you know how much your mother and I love you. You are aware that I had no education while growing up and nor did your mother. You have first-hand experience of what it is like to have parents who are illiterate; it is not a nice thing. I can read but barely, and your mother cannot read at all. We have high hopes that you will go further in life: you will be the most educated person in your entire extended family, and your mother and I are determined to make that become a reality. You know that I retired from business and the only income we have now is from the corner shop that your mother runs; we are hoping that this will be lucrative enough to help us lead a good middle-class life – after all, it is only me, you and your mother, not a large family like your other extended family. We are backing you to do well in school, go to university, and get a good job that will give you and yours a good life.'

The waiter interrupted my Father's counsel. 'Here are your orders, sorry for the delay, but I am glad to say your brown rice is here, sir, and your camel meat is well done. For the young man, here is your order too – enjoy,' he said with a big smile on his face.

My Father continued offering advice while eating his brown rice and camel meat, occasionally stopping to wash down the food with his freshly squeezed mango juice. 'Sahal, the sky is the limit for you: Marka is a good place to study, make the most of what the city can offer, but be mindful that you are here to study and complete your secondary education,' he said. Because my Father was speaking, and I was not required to respond to any particular question, I was both listening and eating. As soon as we had finished our food, my Father asked the waiter for the bill, but was told to go to the counter to pay.

My Father paid, and we left the restaurant. Before we said goodbye, my Father reminded me to go to Luuleey's breakfast club on Fridays and Saturdays and gave me pocket money for the term. I felt a surge of pride and determination. Back in my dormitory that night, I lay in bed, replaying the day's events: my Father's support, Uncle Hudle's shopping offer, Luuleey's generous breakfasts – everything seemed to be falling into place, and it felt like the best day of my life.

My Father left Marka on the following day. On the next Friday, as agreed, I went to Aunt Luuleey's breakfast club, which was open between 7 am and 10 am. I arrived at 8.30 am, when it was very busy but orderly: Aunt Luuleey was sitting at the till; two waiters were taking orders, and in the kitchen, which has an open door to the dining area, three women were busy making pancakes.

'Sahal soo dhawoow Eedo, Sahal, welcome from your aunty,' exclaimed Luuleey. I took a seat near the door. The menus laid out on every table had two sections – breakfast, comprising pancakes, honey, and sesame oil on top, and drinks, which listed sweet tea, either black or with goat's milk. This combination was very popular with the regular customers, and Aunt Luuleey and her team at the breakfast club were content to keep the menu simple. Until the end of the term, the breakfast club was a place I looked forward to all week: Fridays and Saturdays became special days.

I ended the year very well – my grades had improved immensely, I was now academically one of the most respected students in my year group, and I was noticed by my teachers. At the end-of-year ceremony, I was awarded a certificate for being the most improved student of the year.

At the end of each academic year, I would travel back to Baidoa, via Mogadishu, to visit my Mother and Father. While I was there, I would spend time with my childhood friend, Hassanoow, and my middle school friend, Hindiyeey.

Love, Work and the Weight of Family

I Wanted to Earn, Study and Love,
but My Father Only Approved of Studying.

In my second year at Hiloowle boarding school – my Year 10 – I was transformed from an unknown Maay-Maay-speaking, working-class kid from Baidoa into a high-flying student who enjoyed friendships with students from various backgrounds, many of whom were from affluent families.

One morning, while I was having breakfast at Aunt Luuleey's club, a tall, skinny, bald man appeared at the till. Initially, I did not recognise him, but as soon as I heard, 'Luuleey, my sister, how are you, and how is the breakfast business doing?' I knew it was Uncle Hudle. The last time I'd seen him was at the river restaurant. I was supposed to visit his shop, and he was meant to 'keep an eye on me' – neither of which had happened.

Before Aunt Luuleey could respond, Uncle Hudle turned his small head towards the corner where I was sitting. There I was – his nephew, the one he was supposed to be keeping an eye on, but had not.

'Sahal, son of my brother Diinoow, you disappeared! You never showed up at my shop. I'm still waiting for you!' exclaimed Uncle Hudle.

'True, Adeer. I was just busy, buried in schoolwork. But I promise I'll come by next Friday,' I replied, speaking timidly while still chewing a piece of pancake.

'No problem, I'll be waiting for you next Friday. Don't disappear again, young man,' he responded quickly.

As I had promised, the following Friday, after finishing my breakfast, I went straight to Uncle Hudle's shop. When I arrived, he was with a customer, so I decided to wait outside. Once he had served the customer, I stepped inside, but before I could utter a word of greeting, Uncle Hudle called out from behind the till, 'Good day, son of my brother Diinoow! Great to see you coming – welcome, welcome, welcome!'

'Thank you, Uncle. Great to be here,' I replied. Before I could say anything else, he continued, 'Sahal, I've heard you're good with numbers, and I can see you're a trustworthy young man. I'm going to offer you a part-time job. Your Father may not be pleased about it because he wants you to focus on your schoolwork, but it's only one day – Fridays – and it will give you some much-needed experience.' Before I could accept or decline, he added, 'Next Friday is your start date, okay, Adeer? Now, I need to serve the next customer.'

I was not sure what to make of Uncle Hudle's offer. Part of me wanted to earn some pocket money and learn how a business works, but another part wanted to focus on my studies and only work if necessary, during the summer holidays. I stayed in the shop for another hour, partly to see how things ran and partly to consider his offer. After the customers had left, I said, 'Uncle Hudle, I'm here in Marka to attend school, and I've only got one year left before my final Year 12 exams. I'm sorry, but I can't work this year. Next year, though, I'd love to accept your offer.'

After a few moments of silence, Uncle Hudle nodded and said, 'All right, next year it is. The offer still stands. But if you change your mind, you know where to find the shop.'

The academic year ten ended, and I finished with the second-highest marks in my class – an achievement that would set me apart from my peers until the end of secondary education. As usual, I packed my bags and travelled to Baidoa to spend the summer holidays with my Father and mother.

That summer, I learned of the passing of my uncle, the only brother of my Father, to whom I owe the fact that I even knew my birthday. He had returned to his Lord after three months battling pneumonia at Digfeer Hospital in Mogadishu. My Father was distraught for weeks: not only were they brothers who shared the same parents, but they were also best friends. My uncle had supported my Father financially and emotionally throughout his life, and his absence was a heavy loss, felt not just by my Father but also by my mother, who was fond of him.

Despite this tragedy, I managed to have a good summer – playing football, swimming with my friend Hassanoow, and spending time with Hindiyeey. A week before my summer holiday ended, as I began preparing to return to Marka, I heard the shocking news that Hassanoow had decided to drop out of school and take up an apprenticeship at a local auto mechanic workshop. It was hard to believe, considering how academically talented he was. I could not help but wonder whether this was his parents' decision or whether he had chosen this path himself. When I tried to ask, Hassanoow was reluctant to explain, and I decided not to press further.

On the brighter side, I discovered that Hindiyeey's parents had decided to transfer her to Marka, where she would finish Year 11 and Year 12 at Sakhaawadiin, a top-performing girls' grammar school in an affluent area of the city.

While I was disappointed by Hassanoow's decision, I was happy that Hindiyeey – a good friend and, secretly, someone I cared for even more than that – would now be joining me in Marka. Sakhaawadiin was a boarding school like mine, but it charged tuition fees, and only wealthy families could afford to send their daughters there.

The night before my departure, Hindiyeey and her friends invited me to a farewell dinner celebrating her imminent move to Marka. After the meal, she and I left together since our homes were close to one another. On the way back, I noticed that she seemed unusually quiet. She kept looking at me as if she wanted to say something, but could not muster the courage. After a few moments of awkward silence, she finally stopped walking and, with a newfound determination, said, 'Sahal, I have something to tell you.'

'What? Go on, tell me,' I replied, trying to sound calm and encouraging.

'You know ... since that day when our team won the quiz, I kind of ... liked you ...' She hesitated, clearly gathering her thoughts, before continuing, 'And then when you transferred to Hiloowle boarding school in Marka, I started missing you and longing for the summer holidays when you'd return to Baidoa.' She paused again, before blurting out, 'In short, I guess what I want to tell you is ... I have feelings for you.'

I was taken aback. Although I had suspected that she liked me, I had never imagined her feelings were this strong. Searching for a response, I said, 'I ... I, too, have feelings for you.' As soon as the words left my mouth, I knew my heart was not lying, but internally, I was grappling with the reality of our different worlds. Hindiyeey came from a well-to-do upper-middle-class family. Her Father, Jabriil, was a high-ranking bureaucrat, respected and influential. She had the looks – tall, with glowing skin and a face that could captivate anyone who looked at her. She was smart, academically brilliant, and the kind of girl everyone admired.

I, on the other hand, came from a modest background. My parents were illiterate. My Father had neither the ambition nor the opportunity to attain social prominence. I was a Maay-Maay-speaking boy born in Daynuunaay, delivered by my grandmother with no medical tools or training. Hindiyeey, in contrast, was an Af-Mahaa-tiri speaker, born in an Italian-run maternity hospital in Mogadishu before her family moved to Baidoa. We were opposites in every conceivable way, an unlikely pair. We agreed to keep our feelings secret, even while in Marka. It was consistent with the norms of the time; our parents were devout Muslims, and the restrictions on interactions between boys and girls were very stringent. As we said goodbye that night, though, I could not help but feel that life in Marka was about to get much more interesting.

The following day, I travelled to Marka via Mogadishu. On previous trips, my Father would always find someone heading to Marka and ask them to look after me during the journey. However, now that I was older, he trusted me to travel alone. I spent a day with my uncle's family in Mogadishu – a very difficult day, given the recent loss of my uncle, who was deeply loved by so many. Grief hung heavily in the air, making the visit sombre and emotionally draining.

When I finally arrived in Marka, I felt like a very different person. I was older and, perhaps, wiser. This year felt full of potential – I would soon be joined by Hindiyeey, who shared the same feelings that I had for her. And there was also the possibility of starting a job at Uncle Hudle's shop.

The following Friday, I went for breakfast at Aunt Luuleey's breakfast club, as usual. After finishing my breakfast, I headed straight to Uncle Hudle's shop.

'Good day, son of my brother Diinoow!' shouted Uncle Hudle from behind the till as soon as he saw me walk in. Although he knew my first name, he always called me 'the son of my brother Diinoow'. Initially, I found this mildly irritating and resented it. But, as time went on, I realised how much he admired my Father, and I learned to tolerate the nickname – even if I never quite liked it.

'Are you ready to start work with me today?' Uncle Hudle asked, still busy counting a bundle of money.

'No, uncle,' I replied politely. 'I just got back from my summer holiday in Baidoa. I need to know my school timetable for the year first, and then I'll let you know when I can start. But I'd love to work for you this year.'

'Good, that's a sensible idea,' he said, nodding while expertly wrapping a rubber band around the stack of notes. 'Just let me know when you're ready.'

Uncle Hudle's shop was as lively as ever, with customers constantly coming and going, each greeted with his trademark jovial voice: 'Welcome, welcome, welcome!' As I would later realise, Uncle Hudle repeated words three times, either when he was stressed or when he wanted to emphasise something. As I watched him handle his business, I could not help but feel that this year in Marka would be unlike any other.

The following week, I started school and received my new timetable. It was not very different from my Year 10 timetable – I had the same teachers, the same subjects, and more or less the same classrooms. Around this time, Hindiyeey also began her new life at Sakhaawadiin. A few Fridays came and went, and instead of starting my part-time job at Uncle Hudle's shop, I decided to spend time with Hindiyeey, showing her around Marka so that she would not feel out of place. By the fourth week of the academic year, I finally began working at the shop.

At first, the work was fast-paced, and I struggled to keep up with the demands of serving customers, but once I got the hang of it, I was flying, and Uncle Hudle was thrilled. My skills in numeracy and literacy proved invaluable, and he quickly began delegating significant responsibilities to me.

One thing I noticed while working with him was how generous a man he was, both with his money and his words. Struggling customers often came to him, and he never hesitated to help them, either with loans or outright donations. These customers always repaid him and remained fiercely loyal.

After months of working with Uncle Hudle, word reached Baidoa that I was now working at his shop on Fridays. My Father was far from pleased and sent me a letter expressing his displeasure:

Sahal,

Hope you are well. I have just received the distressing news that you have been working at Hudle's shop since the start of your Year 11 academic year. I am not happy about this and cannot fathom what drove you to it. Money? Boredom? Or sheer confusion of priorities? Whatever the reason, I want you to stop immediately, upon reading this letter.

Sahal, you may wonder why I am so opposed to this. The reason is simple: next year, you will sit your final exams. You know how much your mother and I want you to excel and pursue higher education. If you continue doing unnecessary part-time jobs, your studies will suffer. It is a distraction you cannot afford. Stop this immediately.

Your Father

My Father is typically a man of few words and rarely shows much emotion, but the tone of this letter left me in no doubt – he was both angry and deeply disappointed. He did not even start the letter with his usual 'Aabo Sahal', instead beginning with just my name, a clear sign of his frustration.

Like my Father, I rarely show my emotions. I have always been private about matters of the heart and family – a trait I probably inherited from my mother. She never shared her frustrations over my Father's long absences with anyone, not even close friends or family. She guarded fiercely the inner workings of our family life.

The letter touched me deeply. I did not want to give up my part-time job, with its interesting conversations and invaluable lessons, but I also did not want to disappoint my Father, whom I loved dearly. I found myself in a dilemma: I could continue working and upset my Father, or quit the job to please him.

To help make sense of my situation, I turned to the one person I trusted completely with my fears and vulnerabilities – Hindiyeey. She was now the love of my life and my most trusted confidant. Since her arrival in Marka, my social and emotional life had blossomed. She was kind, intelligent, beautiful and spiritually grounded – a person with whom I could share my innermost thoughts without fear of betrayal.

Every Friday after the shop closed and following sunset prayers, I would meet Hindiyeey before heading back to school to prepare for the next day's classes. The Friday after I received the letter, I went straight to meet her after finishing work, not mentioning anything to Uncle Hudle about my Father's letter.

The school halls where Hindiyeey stayed were private and exclusively for girls, with no males allowed. However, there were coffee shops nearby where the students often socialised. One such spot, Baraawe Coffee Shop, was our favourite. It was run by a kind and religious couple of Barawian heritage who were open-minded and understanding of students' needs. They knew about my connection with Hindiyeey and were aware that we were in love, but they understood that we were well-behaved, God-fearing students who had been brought up well.

'Hindiyeey, I need your advice,' I said, my voice carrying a note of urgency.

'What? Is everything okay? You look like you're in a hurry,' she asked, her brow furrowing with concern.

'Yes... erm, yes, everything is okay. But I need you to give me your honest advice – please, honest advice,' I replied, placing the letter on the table between us before she could say another word. 'My Father sent this letter. He's not happy that I'm working with Uncle Hudle. He thinks it's a distraction and wants me to stop. But I love the job – it pays me pocket money, and I enjoy working with Uncle Hudle.'

Hindiyeey, ever a thoughtful and careful speaker, took a moment to process what I had said. She never rushed her responses and always listened carefully before giving her opinion.

'Have you made a decision about what to do, or are you still thinking about it?' she asked.

'No, I haven't decided yet. That's why I need your advice,' I replied.

'Okay,' she began, her voice calm and measured. 'My sincere advice to you is that you should listen to your Father.'

She paused for a moment, then continued, 'You have the opportunity to work during the holidays, so don't risk your good relationship with him. I guess what I'm saying is, stop working for now and focus on your schoolwork.'

I nodded, but before I could respond, she added, 'Sahal, my love, if it's the money, I'm happy to share my allowance with you. My Father sends me a generous amount every month.'

Feeling a sudden wave of embarrassment, I quickly shook my head. 'No, no, it's not about the money. I just... I like the place. And, erm, my Father sends me money too, so I'm good.'

'Okay then,' she said, her voice soft and reassuring. 'Please, love, listen to your Father. He is guiding you towards what's best for you.'

'Okay. Thank you for your advice, love,' I said, feeling some relief.

I had a week to digest Hindiyeey's advice and, strangely, even though I had decided to leave my job, I still harboured a faint hope that my Father might change his mind. Perhaps, I thought, I would receive another letter permitting me to continue my part-time job.

When Friday came, I made my way to Uncle Hudle's shop – not to work, but to hand in my resignation. The night before, my mind had been consumed with endless scenarios of how I would break the news to him. How would I explain this to a man who seemed so genuinely happy with my help at his shop? Would I tell him the truth – that my Father had ordered me to quit? But would that not embarrass my Father and potentially strain the good relationship between them? Or should I lie and say that school was becoming too demanding for me to continue working?

These questions swirled relentlessly in my mind, driving me to the brink of insanity. I went back and forth between options, feeling the weight of the decision. Whatever I chose to say, I knew it would not be easy.

'Good morning, the son of my brother Diinoow! Welcome, welcome, welcome!' Uncle Hudle shouted jovially as soon as I entered the shop.

'Good morning, Uncle,' I replied in a subdued tone, feeling the weight of the conversation I was about to have. 'Uncle, can I talk to you for a second?' I asked hesitantly.

'Yes, what is the matter?' Uncle Hudle replied, sipping his tea, his cheerful demeanour slightly fading as he sensed my unease.

'No, nothing's the matter, but erm... erm...' I stammered, my throat suddenly dry. 'I wanted to tell you that after today ...' I paused, unsure how to continue.

'After today, what?' Uncle Hudle asked, his face now showing concern.

'Because of some personal issues, I will not be able to carry on working with you, Uncle,' I finally blurted out, my words tumbling out in a rush. 'It's not because of anything you've done, or because I don't like working here. Quite the contrary – I love working with you! But it's just ... personal issues that mean I have to stop working.'

By the time I finished, I was sweating, my heart pounding as though I had run a marathon. I could feel my lungs gasping for air as if the weight of my words had physically drained me.

'Sahal,' Uncle Hudle said, and for the first time, he called me by my first name. 'You don't have to be sorry. I understand. After all, you are at school and only 17 years old. I also understand that my brother Diinoow wasn't happy about you taking a part-time job, so there's no need to worry.'

He always referred to my Father as 'brother,' though they were distant cousins rather than siblings.

'Thank you for your understanding, Uncle,' I replied, relieved.

Before I could say anything else, Uncle Hudle stood up, still holding his cup of tea, and said, 'But you will have to work with me today. I need to meet a client, and I need you to look after the shop while I'm away.'

Although I had not planned much for the day apart from meeting Hindiyeey in the evening, I was not expecting him to ask me to stay. Yet, out of relief that he had not seemed too upset about my resignation and had not pressed me for reasons, I said, 'No problem, Uncle. Go and meet your client – I'll take care of the shop. Take your time.'

'Thank you, the son of my brother Diinoow, thank you,' he said warmly, waving goodbye as he left the shop.

Uncle Hudle was away for about three hours. The afternoon was surprisingly quiet, with very few customers coming and going. This was a relief for me, as it gave me space to think and reflect on what I would do with my Fridays now that I would not be working in the shop anymore. Would I spend the entire day with Hindiyeey, or should I find something else to occupy my time?

The stillness of the afternoon also provided an opportunity to write to my Father, letting him know that I had followed his advice–or rather his orders–and had resigned from my part-time job at Uncle Hudle's shop.

My letter read:

Dear Aabo,

I hope you and Hooyo are both well. I am well here in Marka, and school is going well. I am, as always, working hard to achieve good grades. I still go to Aunt Luuleey's breakfast club on Fridays and Saturdays, and everything is fine.

Aabo, I am writing this letter in response to your earlier one. I am sorry for not informing you that I took a part-time job at Uncle Hudle's shop. At the time, my reasoning was twofold: to gain more experience in how business works and to earn some much-needed pocket money to supplement the monthly allowance you send me. However, in hindsight, you are absolutely right, Aabo – there is the potential for this to negatively impact my studies. As you made your stance very clear, I do not want to do anything that could jeopardise my success at school.

In short, I want to let you know that I have taken your advice and resigned from my part-time job. In fact, I am writing this letter while at Uncle Hudle's shop on my last day here. Aabo, please forgive me for my mistake, and I am sorry for keeping you in the dark.

Yours,

Your Son

As I finished writing the letter, Uncle Hudle returned.

'Good evening, the son of my brother Diinoow. How are things? Any issues with customers or products?' he asked as he entered the shop, his voice full of energy.

'No, Uncle, all good. In fact, it was a very quiet afternoon. I only had a couple of customers, and not much else happened,' I replied, quickly sliding the letter out of sight.

'Good, good, good,' he said cheerfully, setting down his bag and taking his seat behind the counter.

I said goodbye to Uncle Hudle, knowing this was likely the last time I would work in his shop, though hopefully not the last time I would visit. Just as I was about to leave, Uncle Hudle said abruptly, 'Sahal, the son of my brother Diinoow, I know today is your last day working with me. But if I am truthful, I am sad that you're leaving. I had hoped you would stay longer. Still, I understand that my brother Diinoow wasn't happy with your part-time job, and I respect that.'

I interjected hastily, 'No, Uncle, it wasn't my Father who made me stop working here.'

I knew I was lying, but I could not let my Father be blamed. I did not want anything to jeopardise the good relationship between him and Uncle Hudle. I just wanted to leave quietly, without creating any tension.

Uncle Hudle continued, 'You know, Sahal, the son of my brother Diinoow, I don't have a son like you. My eldest son is your age, but he's not suited to the world of business. I've tried to train him so he could one day take over the family business, but he has repeatedly failed. He's cost me a lot of money and has deeply disappointed me. For now, I've decided to keep him at arm's length and manage the shop on my own until my younger son, who is only five, grows up.'

As he spoke, I could see the sadness in his eyes. This caught me off guard, and I did not know what to say except, 'I'm sorry, Uncle. I'm really sorry.'

'No, no,' he said, waving his hand dismissively. 'You don't need to be sorry – it's not your fault. My brother Diinoow is a lucky man to have you as his son.'

It was getting late, and the sun was about to set. I remembered I had to meet Hindiyeey at the Baraawe coffee shop, but Uncle Hudle had not finished talking.

'As a Father,' he said, his voice simmering with emotion, 'there's nothing more precious than seeing your child progress in life. My firstborn hasn't shown that progress, and now I worry about the influence he might have on his younger brother.'

'Uncle,' I said gently, feeling restless but not wanting to offend him, 'I'll come back another day so we can talk more. But I need to go now. I'm sorry, Uncle.'

'No, that's fine,' he said, his tone softening. 'I was just sharing my frustration. Here – take this,' he said, handing me some money. 'It's a gift from me to you. Stay blessed, the son of my brother Diinoow. And don't forget – if you need anything, don't disappear, okay?'

'Thank you, Uncle. I appreciate your generosity – thank you again,' I said sincerely before leaving the shop with a heavy heart, not because I had left my job, but feeling genuinely sorry about Uncle Hudle's disappointment with his firstborn son.

By the time I arrived at Baraawe café shop, Hindiyeey had become tired of waiting and was about to leave, as it was getting darker.

'I am so sorry, my love,' I said apologetically.

'That is all right, my love, but what kept you so long? We were meant to meet two hours ago?' asked Hindiyeey.

'I will explain. I am sorry again, but hopefully you will understand.'

'Okay, explain to me,' responded Hindiyeey, while pushing something wrapped in beautiful paper towards me.

'What is this?'

'You will see it in a minute, but tell me why you were late. What held you back?'

'Okay, okay,' I said, with an element of excitement. What was this that was so beautifully wrapped? We had exchanged gifts before, but had never wrapped them. Hiding my excitement about the gift in front of me, I gathered my thoughts and started, 'Hindiyeey, you know today was my last day working at Uncle Hudle's shop. The aim was to go and break the news to him that I could no longer work there. I was very worried about it, but when I explained it to him, I was pleasantly surprised at how well he took the news. I could see in his eyes, though, that he was emotional, and he kept telling me stories about his elder son, which was a bit sad. After we had finished talking, he told me that he had an appointment and asked me to look after the shop in his absence. I am sorry, that is why I am late, but all's well that ends well.'

While I was explaining, Hindiyeey was listening to me attentively. She has always been a good listener; she never interrupts people, but always asks questions in conversation. However, on this occasion, there were some nods and no questions; perhaps she understood it all and had no need to ask any questions, or perhaps she simply had no time to do so since it was late in the evening.

'That is good news. Do you want to unwrap this now?' asked Hindiyeey.

'Sure,' I said, forcing a smile. I unwrapped the gift and after removing a couple of layers of wrapping paper, I reached it – halwa, freshly made, brown, with an aroma of cardamom that

filled the entire room. 'Oh, thank you, my love, who made it?'
I asked.

'You are welcome, my love. I bought it from Halwa Ali-
baba just across the road. I thought you would like it and this
will last you for a week,' said Hindiyeey, enthusiastically.

'Of course, and thank you again. I love it! Can I try it?' I
said, already salivating for the halwa.

'Yes, of course, try it and tell me if you like it. I got some
last week and I loved it.'

'Mmm, it's nice, really nice,' I replied, chewing a good
chunk of the halwa in my mouth.

From Illness to Recovery: A Summer to Remember

The Year I Came Close to Losing Everything.

The remaining part of the academic year ended as well as I could possibly have hoped. Hindiyeey and I had a wonderful time: we saw each other every Friday and Saturday, chatted for hours, grew fond of each other, and openly enjoyed each other's company. When the academic year ended, just as I was preparing to go back to Baidoa, I received a letter from my Father saying that he and my mother were coming to Marka to spend the school holidays as a family, so I needed to stay in Marka and not travel back to Baidoa. This was rather a surprise because I was not expecting to spend my summer holidays in Marka with my Mother and Father. Although the prospect of seeing my mother in Marka and showing her around the city – a place that had been my home for the last three years – was very appealing, deep down I knew that Hindiyeey would be out of town and spending her holidays in Baidoa with her family.

The same week that Hindiyeey left for Baidoa, my Mother and Father arrived in Marka. The day before they arrived, I went to Uncle Hudle's shop to say hello and tell him that my Father and Mother were on their way to Marka to spend the school holidays with me. 'Here comes the son of my brother Diinoow – how nice to see you!' Uncle Hudle shouted from behind the till.

'How are you, Uncle?' I asked in a less carrying voice.

'Good, good,' said Uncle Hudle, and before I could say another word, he shouted again, 'I heard my brother Diinoow and my sister Suleey are coming to Marka.'

Surprised, I asked, 'Yes, Uncle, but how did you know that?'

'Ah, because Diinoow sent me a message asking me to find a house for the three of you to stay during the school holidays, and I found a nice house, perfect for the three of you to stay in,' replied Uncle Hudle.

'Oh, thank you, Uncle, that is very kind of you, but where is the house located, may I ask?' I promptly enquired.

'Not far from where I live. It is in a nice neighbourhood; I am sure you will love it... I've got the key here, look,' said Uncle Hudle.

'That's nice to know, uncle,' I said, as I waved goodbye. The following day, as expected, my parents arrived in Marka from Baidoa. This was the first time that we had been together as a family in Marka, and, thanks to my parents renting a good and spacious house in a well-to-do neighbourhood, I had the best school holiday ever. Almost every day, my parents and I would go to the sea; I would swim, and they would sit at the edge of the water dipping their toes in the waves. After each visit to the beach, I would take them to different seafood restaurants so that we could have freshly fried fish with brown rice. One of these restaurants was Ali-Bihi's, named after its owner, an old man in his late seventies with no children. Ali-Bihi served his customers with gusto and always had a big smile. 'Soo dhawaada, soo dhawaada, Welcome, welcome,' was his motto. His restaurant was always busy, mainly with customers visiting the seafront. My parents, especially my Father, fell in love with Ali-Bihi's fried fish and brown rice and would always thank him after we ate lunch.

Just two weeks before the academic year was due to start and one day after Hindiyeey had arrived back in Marka from her holiday break in Baidoa, I was struck down by pneumonia. As the days passed, my illness worsened. My parents decided to take me to Marka's main hospital, but the doctors there advised them to take me to Mogadishu, where there were better medical facilities to treat my illness, which was becoming serious. My parents were panic-stricken; losing a child is very painful for any parents, and my being an only child added more stress and urgency.

My parents had spent their budget for the holiday and had not planned any contingency for the medical bills and hospitalisation costs if we went to Mogadishu. After consulting another doctor, my parents decided to take me to a pneumonia specialist in Mogadishu. Although healthcare was at that time free to all Somali citizens, the system was in a parlous state, so people often opted for private healthcare. Of course, not everyone could afford this, and my parents were not necessarily financially well off. However, for the last few years, my mother's corner shop had been doing so well that my parents had some savings.

Hindiyeey was distraught to see that I was very ill and would probably miss the start of my Year 12, or even potentially the entire year. She could see that I was losing weight fast, that I was not eating, and that my parents were worried about the state of my health. She was worried on finding out that I would be transported to Mogadishu to see a specialist. My parents managed to get a private ambulance to take me to Mogadishu and, on the following day, a family friend who had worked with my late uncle in Mogadishu hired a taxi to take me to the pneumonia specialist in the Waberi district, where I spent the day undergoing various tests with a nurse before seeing the doctor for the results. From the waiting room, the nurse called us into the doctor's office, where an old man wearing thick glasses sat, surrounded by piles of medical files, with a typewriter and a large medical book to his right and two chairs for visiting patients to his left. To our surprise, he knew my late uncle and was aware that he had a brother in Baidoa. He read the results to us, including from the X-ray, and recommended that I take a course of antibiotics and multivitamins for three months and then return to him for a check-up.

'Doctor, my son goes to school in Marka, and term starts next week. Can he take his medication while attending school?' my mother asked the doctor.

'No, you have to understand that your son is very poorly; in fact, the pneumonia he has is so severe that he may need further treatment after the three months so there will no school for your son for a minimum of four months.'

I could hear my Father's deep sigh next to me, and my mother was lost for words. 'Four months?' she repeated.

'Yes, and that is a conservative estimate; it may be more,' said the doctor, adjusting his thick glasses. I was too weak and disoriented to even think coherently, let alone to join in the conversation.

My Father took a deep breath and said to my mother, 'The school can wait, we need to get our son back on track, his health is our priority now.' My mother nodded, feeling dejected. We left the doctor's office with a long list of medical prescriptions for the next three months.

After two weeks of taking the medication, my health started to improve dramatically. I was no longer so weak; I started eating well and had more energy, but I had to follow the doctor's advice and finish the course of medication.

After three months of antibiotics, my health had returned to normal. We saw the doctor for a check-up, and my parents and I were pleased when he gave me a clean bill of health, with the caveat that I needed to rest for at least one more month before I went back to school. My parents agreed to his recommendation but requested that he give them a doctor's letter so that my school would be notified that my extended absence was due to ill health.

While I was recovering in Mogadishu, Hindiyeey kept sending me letters of encouragement, love, and prayers. Every letter she sent ended, '.... I pray to Allah to give you good health and to enable us to meet again in Marka sooner.' This line became her signature in every letter she sent and was written indelibly in my heart, giving me a source of energy, a ray of hope that I would, with Allah's help, get back to Marka and meet Hindiyeey sooner. After four months of illness in Mogadishu, I returned to Marka, feeling healthier and with new energy.

While it was good to be back in Marka, I faced the daunting prospect of catching up on four months of schoolwork in the final year of my secondary education – Form Four, as it is widely known. In school, and in anything to do with school, I had always done well, found it easy to learn, remember lessons, and recall information in tests. In that respect, I was, therefore, as confident as I could be, but the reality was that I had not opened a book or read anything for four months. Hindiyeey was delighted to see me back, and my other friends, too, were pleased to see me back healthy and ready to finish the year. Uncle Hudle was keen to be in touch and help me in any way he could because of my disrupted studies. Luuleey, the distant cousin of my mother who ran the breakfast club, also offered me free Friday and Saturday breakfasts for the rest of the year. After my first week back in Marka, the old me – me, the person I was before the illness struck–was back. I was happy, full of energy, with a smile on my face and a spring in my stride. As my exams were not far off, Hindiyeey suggested that I should spend more time studying than meeting up.

'Sahal, you have lost a lot of school days, not of course through any fault of yours, but because you were ill. I want you to study harder; I am happy to meet with you occasionally, and I understand,' said Hindiyeey, holding my hand.

'I will, you are right, time is not on my side, and I thank you for your encouragement,' I said, looking at her tenderly. Hindiyeey was also preparing for her final exams in Year 12, but she was as calm as anyone could be. She was, by nature, a very confident student and had always performed academically better than all her classmates. In addition to her academic work ethic, she maintained her religious devotion, reading the Quran, praying until the small hours of the morning, and always carrying herself modestly.

With that advice, I went into study mode, seeing Hindiyeey sometimes once a week but usually only fortnightly. Our meetings would be brief, conscious of the need to study, but very pleasant and full of love. After four months of sleepless nights, the exams came and went. Afterwards, I felt exhausted and weak but in high spirits. After all, a few months earlier, I had been so ill that I was not sure whether I would return to school to finish the year. I was not even sure whether I would ever even return to Marka because of the severity of my illness, but here I was, having completed my exams for Year 12, and happy with how they had gone.

Hindiyeey's exams had gone well too; she felt she had performed well in them and was also in high spirits. The weekend following the end of the exams, the school invited all the students in the cohort and their friends to a dinner with the principal and the Head of Year. I invited Hindiyeey, and we both attended the dinner; for Hindiyeey to be in my school and meeting all my classmates felt surreal but very memorable. One week later, it was time for Hindiyeey and me to say goodbye to Marka, a city very dear to both of us, the city that had been home to me for four years and that was now full of precious memories for us both. It was, after all, in Marka that we grew closer, that we truly fell in love and promised to care for and love one another. Hindiyeey was the first to leave for Baidoa via Mogadishu, and I left three days later because the travel money my Father sent to me was delayed. When I received the money from Juunoow, who had a shop in Marka and via whom my Father always used to send my monthly living allowance, he gave me a short letter, only one paragraph long, from my Father.

'Son, very well done for completing the exams we thought you would never complete, all praise is to Allah, the Lord of the

Universe. Son, go via Mogadishu and do some shopping for yourself and use the money – it is all yours. Your Father and mother.'

This note was very strange on two fronts: first, it was unusually short – my Father was in the habit of writing, or rather dictating, long letters; and secondly, he always advised me to be frugal in spending my pocket money. However, reading the note closely, I could feel my Father's happiness and pride at the occasion. I went to Mogadishu from Marka on the following day, and spent two days there buying summer clothes before travelling to Baidoa to begin the anxious three months' wait for my exam results.

Part II – Exile

The Collapse

*The World We Knew Crumbled in an Instant, and With It,
Everything We Held Dear Slipped into the Unknown.*

When the results came out, we were both proud: I got 63%
and Hindiyeey 94% – top of her entire year group. In a normal
year, my result would have been average and disappointing,
but this was not a normal year for me. I had only had four
months of schooling; I was ill for the first four months of the
academic year and still psychologically tired when I took the
exams. In the last two weeks leading up to the exams, I had
sleepless nights, nightmares and sweaty palms, but we both
worked hard, dreaming not just of successfully completing our
secondary education, but of going on to higher education and
a shared life afterwards. It was national policy that all high-
school graduates must complete two years of national service.
Hindiyeey and I chose to serve in the education sector rather
than the police or the territorial army, which were the other
options. Teaching made sense for us as we both loved books,
children and the idea of shaping minds, so we were sent to
Halane, in Mogadishu, to train as primary school teachers.

For a time, life felt certain, even joyful. We lived in a shared
compound with other trainees, and although we were not
allowed to live together, we stole time together in the library
and in the courtyards, where the wind carried the scent of the
ocean on a cool breeze in the evening and at sunset. We
whispered our dreams to each other: a small house in Marka,

our parents and loved ones not far away, a classroom where we could teach side by side, a child or two with her eyes and my nose.

Then everything changed.

Without warning, her family decided that she would marry her cousin, a man she barely knew, who lived and worked in Saudi Arabia. They believed it was best for her. The man had money. He could send money home, build a house for her, pay for a large wedding, and look after their future offspring well. To them, this was security, and she had to marry him.

To us, it was a death sentence: a quiet, bloodless kind that killed not the body but the soul.

When she told me the news, we were sitting under a neem tree in the teacher's garden. She could not look at me. Her voice trembled, as if she were apologising for something she had not done.

'I don't want this,' she whispered. 'But I can't say no. But I also can't say yes to something I know that my heart is against.' I was lost for words. I pretended not to have heard the news, refused to believe what I was hearing; my mind was racing to I knew not where, my knees were shaking and buckling under the weight of the news. After not saying a word for ten minutes, just staring, we simultaneously started crying—not loudly, not theatrically, but with the aching quiet of people who knew their hearts were breaking and could do nothing about it. That week, she stopped coming to classes. The wedding was being prepared, she said, and her cousin was due to arrive in Mogadishu in just a few weeks.

But before he could arrive, before the wedding could happen, history itself intervened. The stars were not aligned for this meeting of cousins; other events were to unfold before it took place. Somalia collapsed.

Like a building struck by an earthquake, the entire nation crumbled overnight. The government fell. Warlords rose. Neighbours turned into enemies. Schools, hospitals, libraries – all were emptied, then looted, then burned.

Within a month of the government being overthrown, Mogadishu became a battleground.

One morning, we woke to the sound of gunfire so close that it shook the windowpanes. My Father, who had come to visit me, pulled me out of Halane before sunset. 'We must leave,' he said. 'We'll head to Baidoa; your mother and your great-aunt are waiting for us. From there, maybe Kenya.' He whispered that Hindiyeey's uncle, who lived in the Madina district of the city, had whisked her away already.

When my Father and I arrived in Baidoa, which was at the time in relative stability, I tried to find her. I went to her family's home, but it had been abandoned. I asked neighbours, but no one knew where they had gone. In the chaos, people disappeared like smoke. Baidoa, too, was starting to empty of its residents; local militia and vigilante groups were gathering everywhere, lynching the clans associated with the old regime. Perhaps Hindiyeey had never arrived back from Mogadishu; perhaps her family had fled the country before she left Mogadishu with her uncle… My thoughts were in such a spin that I could not formulate the possibilities of what might have become of her. That was the last time for years that I heard her name spoken aloud by anyone else, although it was constantly within me, in my thoughts, in my soul, which was desperate to find her in a country now drowning in a tsunami of destruction.

Shadows Across the Border – The Long Walk to the Abyss

We only stayed in Baidoa for three days. My mother, Suleey, and my Great-Aunt Sonkoreey were anxious and kept encouraging my Father to move us all out of Baidoa. When we did leave Baidoa and cross into Kenya, it was no ordinary journey – it was an escape. We left with nothing but a few clothes, some dried food, and memories that felt heavier than our bags. Baidoa had become a ghost town. We walked for days, hitchhiked when we could, and bribed militia and vigilante groups with what little we had.

At the border, there were thousands of us – mothers clutching babies, elders muttering prayers, children too shocked to cry. We were transported to newly formed refugee camps –Dadaab, Dagahaley, Hagadera and Ifo – places that would become the only geography we knew for years. My family and I were finally settled in Dadaab, which would later become the biggest refugee camp in the region.

Life in the camp was about survival: we queued for water, fought for food rations and slept with one eye open. Two weeks into our new life in Dadaab, my Great-Aunt Sonkoreey fell ill, initially suffering from what appeared to be diarrhoea and vomiting. Even when that stopped, she became increasingly weak, fragile and bedridden. Three months later, she passed away peacefully, surrounded by the three of us. My mother was hit hard by the death of her aunt; the grief of losing her second mother weighed heavily on her. For two days, my mother, naturally of a stoic outlook, and patient through life's ups and downs, was hit by an unbearable wave of grief caused by the loss of my great-aunt.

After a year in the camp, we accepted life as it was but not as we would like it to be, and remarkably, we seemed to be happy again. My mother started helping neighbours, teaching the other women how to use a sewing machine and helping them to mend their children's clothing. My Father, too, seemed to have made some friends in the camp and generally appeared to be happy with his newly found circle. In contrast, I found life in the camp very difficult, my nights disrupted by constant dreams of Hindiyeey. I imagined she was still alive. I pictured her somewhere – maybe in Saudi Arabia, maybe still in Mogadishu, maybe married, maybe not. The only news we had of home in Baidoa, of Mogadishu, or Southern Somalia more widely was of destruction, death, and famine. The foreign media, CNN in particular, regularly showed men with guns, looted buildings, dead bodies in the streets, and images of malnourished children and elderly people. Baidoa was hit particularly hard, and scores of people died every day from hunger and a lack of basic food, despite efforts by the international community to distribute food aid.

On the political front, there was no politics, there was no government, there was no rule of law. Neighbours turned on neighbours in the name of their clans; even those who had married into other clans were not safe – an uncle was unable to save from his own clan militia his nephews and nieces who were of a different clan. In Mogadishu, marauding thugs went from house to house, killing members of other clans, especially those associated with the regime. The leaders of the armed groups who had helped overthrow the government were now, after one year of total chaos, fighting one another. Those who were, on paper, from the same clan were fighting each other for power and territory. The international community was hopeless in distributing food aid in the beginning; then came the US intervention, which created more chaos and deep-seated division between the Somalis who wanted foreigners to help and those who did not.

In Kenya and other neighbouring countries, camps full of Somalis fleeing the civil war popped up on every inch of free land. These countries – Kenya, Ethiopia, and Djibouti – struggled to cope with the influx of Somalis fleeing from the grip of death and hunger in their own country.

In Dadaab, remarkably, life was stable: there was food, there was peace because we were in Kenya, and there was a sense of gratitude that we were the lucky ones in having escaped from Somalia and its daily death toll.

In the Classroom of the Displaced

To pass the time and build some sense of normality in my life, I volunteered to teach primary-aged children in the camp literacy and numeracy; after all, I had been training to become a primary school teacher before the calamity struck in Somalia. Makeshift schools were organised and funded by UNICEF and Save the Children; volunteers were not paid wages but were given a small allowance to cover their lunch expenses, and were also provided with the pedagogical training and resources needed to teach the pupils. I continued to volunteer for six months before being promoted to a permanent paid position, training new and in-service volunteers. My parents were so pleased when I told them that I was now a paid UNICEF employee, training those volunteering to teach primary school children. After saving for a few months, I was able to buy a sewing machine for my mother so that she could continue to teach young girls basic sewing and tailoring skills. While in this job, I had access to a number of facilities, including a phone and the UN network, which enabled me to apply for various other jobs, mainly in the education sector and translation. I also improved my English language skills and became quite at ease in my ability to use English in a professional context.

While I was in Nairobi for a week of middle-management training, a visitor came from UNDP – an agency responsible for the United Nations' development programmes – offering interviews for a sought-after scholarship programme in

Germany. They were looking for young men and women with teaching experience and leadership potential. I did not feel qualified for such a scholarship, and had little hope of success, but, nevertheless, I applied for the position, thinking I had nothing to lose. I completed various forms and submitted a two-page personal statement about my life journey and why I thought I would be the best candidate for the scholarship. There were only ten places, but according to the UNDP officer – a middle-aged, silver-haired man with a trimmed goatee beard – there would be other scholarship opportunities if I were unsuccessful in this one, as there was funding available.

Part III – Flight

Against All Odds,
a Flight to the Future

After four months of waiting to find out what had become of my scholarship application, I received a letter from UNDP's regional office in Nairobi, a letter I never dreamt of reading, a letter that opened doors. I had been accepted.

'Dear Mr. Sahal,

We are pleased to inform you that you have been selected for the UNDP School Leadership Fellowship, a highly competitive one-year programme designed to equip exceptional individuals with the skills and knowledge required to lead educational initiatives in crisis-affected regions. Your application stood out for its vision, resilience, and unwavering commitment to improving educational outcomes for refugee children.

As part of this prestigious award, UNDP will cover your full tuition and training fees in Frankfurt, Germany. In addition, the scholarship includes monthly stipends for living expenses, full accommodation, and comprehensive health insurance throughout your stay. To facilitate your travel, you will be provided with two fully funded round-trip airline tickets to and from Frankfurt.

We are confident that upon completion of this programme, your leadership will play a vital role in strengthening education systems in Dadaab Refugee Camp and beyond. Please accept our heartfelt congratulations, and we look forward to supporting you on this journey of impact and transformation.'

I was speechless. I did not know what to say. I could not believe that I was going to Germany to study. I could not believe I was leaving Dadaab for Frankfurt.

I ran back home to break the news to my parents. 'Aabo, Hooyo, I have news for you,' I called, a big smile on my face. Without waiting for their reply, I shouted, 'I'm going to Germany! I've been accepted for the scholarship I applied for four months ago!'

My Father was the first to respond: 'All praise is due to the Lord of the Universe,' he said. My mother followed, also praising Allah, then saying, 'Mabruuk, Hooyo.' After I read the letter to them, they were both delighted yet, at the same time, anxious, anxious about my travel to a foreign country, and the very real possibility that I might not return, that we might not see each other again.

I was told I had one week to prepare for my departure and should report to the UNDP office in Nairobi two days before my scheduled flight on the 8th of October 1993.

While I was happy that I had been granted this opportunity to study in Germany, I shared my parents' anxiety. I was going to a place I knew nothing about, and I was leaving my two elderly parents behind in a refugee camp. I was also anxious about saying goodbye to Hindiyeey. Although I had not heard anything about her whereabouts in over two years, the fact that I was still in Kenya had always given me hope that someday, somehow, I might hear something – whether she was dead or alive.

Three days before I left Dadaab for Nairobi on the first stage of my journey to Frankfurt, my Father slaughtered a goat and invited his friends to celebrate my scholarship and imminent departure. A few prayers were said over lunch by his guests. Later, after everyone had left, my Father and mother called me in to talk to them. After offering a few prayers of their own, they offered me a few pieces of advice.

My Father began, 'Aabo Sahal, first, we want you to stay safe wherever you are. Your mother and I are very happy that you have this opportunity, but naturally, we're anxious. You're a young man, and you're going to a foreign land. The land you're heading to is not a Muslim land. The culture and the way of life are very different from our own.' His voice changed, and I could see the emotion on his face. My mother sat listening, deeply attentive. 'We're getting old. You're our only child. Our future now rests on your shoulders.'

Then my mother took her turn to speak. 'We don't see ourselves staying in Dadaab forever. Hopefully, in the near future, we'll have enough resources to move out of the camp.'

'I absolutely agree, Hooyo,' I interjected.

She nodded and continued. 'Obviously, we don't have the resources now, but we're hopeful this scholarship will give you the opportunity to earn enough in Germany and send something back to support us.'

My Father interjected, 'We're very much hopeful that you'll be the one to get us out of here.'

The night before my departure was full of emotion. My parents shed some tears – and I cried, too, when I saw theirs.

On the following morning, I left for Nairobi to prepare for my journey to Frankfurt. After two days in Nairobi, mostly spent at a hotel organised by the UNDP office, the time to fly finally arrived. When I boarded the plane to Frankfurt, I had ten dollars in my pocket. I was wearing a second-hand shirt and shoes that were too small. I carried only one thing that truly belonged to me: a dream – to better myself, to help my parents move out of Dadaab, and to one day reconnect with the love of my life. In reality, though, I was not sure that any of these dreams could ever come true. I did not know whether I would ever see Hindiyeey again, or whether I would ever have enough to help my ageing parents move to Nairobi or

Garissa. But still, I had to dream. I had to fight. I had to remain positive. And above all, I had to be patient.

After an eight-hour flight, I arrived in Frankfurt. It was early October, mid-autumn, and the air felt uncomfortably chilly against my skin. The airport was buzzing with activity and made me quite dizzy, mostly because I had never experienced anything like a European airport before. My sponsors were waiting for me and, after collecting my luggage, I was met by Eduardo, a Brazilian-born taxi driver who worked for the organisation sponsoring my scholarship. While I was excited, I was also exhausted, and the last thing I wanted was to engage in conversation, but Eduardo was eager to know more about me.

As soon as I got into his car – a well-used white Mercedes-Benz – he shouted, 'Sprechen Sie Deutsch? Do you speak German?'

Not fully understanding the question, I replied, 'I beg your pardon?'

'Oh! No German, just English,' came the instant reply, followed by, 'I speak little English.'

'No problem,' I said, feeling slightly relieved.

On the way to my student accommodation, Eduardo did not stop talking.

'Are you from Kenya? You don't look Kenyan,' he asked.

'No, I'm Somalian, but I currently live in Kenya,' I responded.

Without being asked, Eduardo began to share his own story.

'I was born in Rio, grew up there, and then decided to move to Germany because my former wife was German,' he said. 'But unfortunately, we're not together anymore – we're separated.'

His voice cracked.

'We have two beautiful boys, but they live with her. I only see them once a week, though I pay high child maintenance.'

I was still processing this information, being completely unfamiliar with German or European family court systems, when he suddenly changed the subject.

'Are you married?'

'No,' I said.

'Are you intending to marry?' he asked.

'Yes, one day… but I don't know,' I replied, trying to sound defensive in the hope it would end the conversation so I could get some much-needed rest.

But Eduardo had not finished.

'I would never advise you to marry a European woman – Germans in particular. They'll use you when they need you and throw you under the bus when you're no longer useful to them.'

I nodded silently, offering no verbal response.

'Find your own kind when you're ready,' he added.

We finally arrived at my accommodation. I was tired from the long-haul flight and mentally drained by Eduardo's relentless questions. As I got out of the taxi, a tall, blond, blue-eyed man standing outside waved at me, gesturing for me to come over. I waved back and walked towards him.

'Guten Morgen, Willkommen in Deutschland. Ich heiße Hansel – Good morning, and welcome to Germany. I'm Hansel,' he said, offering me a firm handshake.

'Good morning, sir,' I replied with a smile.

In perfect English, he introduced himself as the head of student welfare, responsible for helping foreign students like me settle in. He had been working for the German Ministry of Education for the last ten years. After we had completed some paperwork, he walked me to my room and handed me the key.

'Here's the room that will be your bedroom for the year you're here,' he said.

'Thank you,' I replied.

'Unpack your luggage and take some rest. I'll be back at one pm sharp to take you to the canteen for lunch,' he said, waving goodbye.

'Sure. Thanks, and see you then,' I said. At one o'clock, I heard a knock on my door. I bolted out of bed, still half-asleep, and opened the door. Hansel stood there, smiling.

'Are you ready, Sahal? Or do you need another ten minutes to get ready?' he asked, peering at me with a knowing smile.

I was still in my pyjamas, eyes bleary from a restless nap. 'Give me five minutes, please?' I blurted out, embarrassed.

'No problem,' Hansel said kindly. 'I'll be back in ten.'

As soon as he walked away, I shut the door and rushed to the shower. I brushed my teeth, dressed quickly, and, by the time Hansel returned, I was already waiting for him outside, trying to look more refreshed than I felt.

We headed to the administration building to finish a few more formalities. Afterwards, we went to the canteen for lunch. The dining hall was not full, with just a handful of international students scattered across the tables, speaking in different languages, their voices blending into a low hum of accents and laughter.

As we joined the queue for food, a short, bald, stocky man, probably in his late twenties, approached us with a wide grin. He had a bold presence and an unmistakable Nigerian accent. 'Hansel! Who's this new face?' he called out warmly.

Hansel smiled and replied, 'This is Sahal, a new student. He's from Kenya.'

'Hello, brother!' the man said, extending his hand with enthusiasm.

'Hello, nice to meet you,' I replied, shaking his hand with a smile.

'My name is Olu,' he said proudly, 'and I've been here for two years. Welcome to Germany!'

Olu seemed to know Hansel well – they joked and exchanged a few words in German. Then Hansel turned to me and said, 'I think it would be a good idea if Olu gave you a short tour of the neighbourhood after lunch. He can also show you the local supermarket and help you get a few things for your room.'

'That would be great,' I said, relieved at the thought of having someone to guide me through this unfamiliar place.

Lunch was simple but filling – rice, steamed vegetables and a piece of grilled chicken. The canteen staff were polite, and the atmosphere felt welcoming, even though everything still felt surreal to me.

After we finished eating, Olu took me around the local area. He was friendly, talkative and seemed to know everyone. He pointed out the nearest bus stop, the pharmacy, the post office and, most importantly, the supermarket where I could buy essentials. I bought some bottled water, fruit, a loaf of bread and toothpaste – basic things to get me through my first few days.

All the while, Olu kept chatting, telling me about life as a student in Germany, the challenges that winter brought, and funny anecdotes from his early days here. I appreciated his warmth, even though I was too tired to take in all the details.

After a couple of hours, we returned to my room. Olu gave me a firm pat on the back and said, 'We'll talk again, brother. Just knock on my door if you need anything. Room 212.' He waved goodbye and disappeared down the hall. Hansel, who had been quiet for most of the walk back, shook my hand and said, 'Get some rest, Sahal. Tomorrow is your big day.'

I nodded. 'Thank you, Hansel. I really appreciate your help.'

'You're welcome,' he said with a smile, then turned and left.

Alone in my room, I sat on the edge of the bed. My new surroundings still felt foreign, but something had shifted. I did not feel completely lost anymore. I felt a sense of stability – something I had not truly experienced for a very long time.

Here I was, sitting in a nicely furnished, warm room in Germany, safe at last from the constant fear of hunger, the terror of war, and the despair of refugee camp life. It was almost surreal. Even this comfort, though, was pierced by a sharp, unsettling thought: my two elderly parents were still trapped in that desperate life of hunger, war, and displacement. While I had escaped to this peaceful refuge, they remained behind, vulnerable and uncertain of what tomorrow might bring. This thought lingered with me as I sat on the bed and, for a moment, the warmth of the room felt distant.

That night, however, I had the best sleep I had enjoyed in many years. It was deep, uninterrupted, and healing. I woke up early, feeling unusually refreshed. After performing my Fajr prayer, I took a long, hot shower and made myself a good, strong cup of tea. The morning was crisp, and a sense of calmness filled the air.

At exactly 8 am, I heard a knock at my door. Before I could even get up, I heard Hansel's familiar voice greeting my next door neighbour. I quickly went to open the door. There he was, standing confidently, wearing the same jacket he had worn the previous day. 'Good morning, Sahal,' he said in his husky, commanding voice.

'Good morning, sir,' I replied, straightening up instinctively.

'Get ready, I will take you to a local doctor for a quick medical check-up. After that, we'll head to the training institute for enrolment and other administrative tasks.'

I was immediately filled with excitement. Throughout my adult life, I had suffered from a persistent stomach ulcer, something I had silently endured for years. The thought of finally seeing a doctor filled me with hope.

On our way to the doctor, we stopped at the canteen for breakfast. The food was delicious – fresh bread, warm eggs, and hot tea. I could already feel my body responding positively to the new environment. At the clinic, I spent nearly two hours with the doctor. He was elderly, calm, and spoke fluent English. He listened attentively as I explained my symptoms and, after a thorough check-up, gave me a tablet for my ulcer and took several blood tests to ensure I was otherwise healthy. For the first time in a long while, I felt like someone was taking my health seriously.

After the appointment, Hansel mentioned that he had another commitment that afternoon but had arranged for Olu to meet me later at the institute and escort me back to the student accommodation. Hansel dropped me at the reception area of the training institute and informed the receptionist – a mixed-race girl with sharp features and a calm energy – that I was there to enrol. He told her I needed to see Catherina, the head of the overseas students' programme, and I sat in the waiting area as she made a few phone calls to locate Catherina, who arrived shortly afterwards, with a bright smile. She was a petite brunette with a joyful face that seemed to light up the room.

'Hello, you must be Sahal,' she said warmly, stretching out her left hand to greet me. Later, I would realise she was left-handed – a detail I found oddly endearing.

'Yes, I am Sahal. How do you do?' I replied politely.

'I'm fine, thank you,' she said, her smile unwavering.

After briefly checking some paperwork, she invited me to follow her to her office on the third floor. It was small but cosy, with a well-organised bookshelf and a clean, tidy desk. A desk lamp was switched on, casting a warm glow over her workspace. She offered me coffee, but I politely declined. She explained the enrolment process and handed me a few documents to sign. One was the bursary agreement: I would receive a monthly bursary of 350 marks, paid on the 25th of every month, unless this fell on a weekend, in which case I would be paid on the preceding Friday. I learnt that I would attend classes four days a week, from 8.45 am to 4 pm, and that a student shuttle bus would be available every hour between the accommodation and the institute.

After completing the paperwork, Catherina walked me to the ID registration office, where I received my student ID card.

She then gave me a short tour of the classrooms and the library. Her enthusiasm was contagious.

'Congratulations, you are now a student at our institute,' she said with another radiant smile. 'Your induction classes begin next Monday. Please be punctual – and good luck!'

'Thank you! I'm so excited,' I blurted, unable to contain my eagerness.

She walked me back to reception, where I was to wait for Olu, who would accompany me back to the accommodation. Fortunately, Olu was already there, animatedly chatting with the receptionist, both of them laughing and exchanging jokes.

'Hi Sahal, you done?' he asked, in his thick Nigerian accent.

'Yes, brother, I am. Thank you,' I replied.

'Before we go, let me introduce you – this is Angel,' he said, pointing to the receptionist. 'She is our sister. Her Father is Eritrean and her mother is German.'

'Oh, nice to meet you, Angel. I'm Sahal, from Somalia,' I said.

Angel shook my hand with a friendly smile. 'Nice to meet you, Sahal.'

We left the institute and boarded the shuttle bus back to the student accommodation. During the 20-minute ride, Olu gave me a passionate and unfiltered lecture about life in Germany. He spoke of what to avoid, what to embrace, and how to navigate this unfamiliar land as a Black foreign student. In those few minutes, he gave me not only advice but a window into his lived experience.

Olu was born in Jos, a city in Nigeria's north-central region. His family had moved to Lagos when he was five. His late Father had been a civil servant working for the Nigerian Federal Inland Revenue, and his mother had died when he was an infant; he had been raised by a kind stepmother whom his Father married a few years after his mother's death. He also had three half-sisters.

Olu had done exceptionally well in school and was awarded a scholarship to study in Germany. Despite his academic success, however, his time in Germany had been marked by hardship. He had faced racist abuse, including a terrifying physical assault at a bus stop by what he called 'skinhead hooligans'. That incident had shaped his worldview, leading to his frequent outbursts: 'Brother, all Germans are white bastards.' It was a sweeping and bitter generalisation, and I soon realised that his deep resentment stemmed from personal trauma.

Although on the surface, Olu and I were both Black African students in Frankfurt, we carried very different ideas of identity. For me, coming straight from East Africa, identity was framed through the lens of clan, not race. I came from a country devastated by civil war – a place where your clan could either save your life or mark you for death. Race had never been a factor in my understanding of self or others. I did not yet understand Olu's anger or his fixation on race. His hostility puzzled me at first, but I would eventually come to understand the depth of pain that underpinned it.

We arrived back at the student accommodation just before supper. After sharing a simple meal in the common area, I thanked Olu sincerely for his time, his stories, and the guidance he had shared.

'Thank you, brother. I really appreciate everything today.'

'No worries, brother,' he said with a grin.

My Induction:
Kindness in a Foreign Tongue

The following Monday, I woke up early, performed my Fajar prayer, read the Holy Quran, and said some supplications in silence. I was wearing a good and warm jacket, which I had bought on Sunday with Olu's help; my old shoes and trousers had also been replaced by a new pair of shoes and trousers gifted by the German Red Cross, which helps new students with winter clothes. The canteen at the student accommodation opened for breakfast at 7 am on weekdays and 8 am on weekends, and by the time I arrived, it was full of students, some of whom must have been queuing before it was opened. Some, like me, were on their induction day; others were students in their first, second, or third years. I tried to find Olu, but he was not there. I had the same breakfast I had had every day since I arrived: toast with butter and jam, boiled eggs, and tea with milk. I was conscious that my induction was due to start at 8.45 am, so I hurried my breakfast and caught the 7.45 am shuttle to the institute. It was a sunny day, but chilly with a light easterly breeze. I arrived at the institute after a mere 20-minute ride. As I had had a campus tour with Catherina in the previous week, I knew where to go for my classes, and at 8.45 am sharp, I was seated in room FB101, waiting for the teacher to arrive. The class was small, only fifteen students; half of these were German and the other half a mixture of South American and Eastern European. To my surprise, I was the only African or Black student there. While Olu would have been bothered by this lonely experience, I did not find it intimidating; in fact, it encouraged me to do well for my own sake and the sake of the continent I represented. My induction left me in high spirits. I was given my timetable for the academic year: I had three classes with Julie on Mondays; two classes and one tutorial with Irma on Tuesdays; three classes with Rolf on Wednesdays; and four classes with Gunther, who was also my personal tutor, on Thursdays. I had Fridays off. The course was assessed through end-of-unit assignments and then an end-of-year project in which students were required to write a project on an educational topic.

Those first weeks settled into a rhythm that I had not expected, almost like the quiet ticking of a clock in a room full of unfamiliar furniture. I was still learning how to sit in this new space – a world of lectures, assignments, and academic curiosity delivered in a language and method foreign to me – but I was not unhappy. The intellectual world I entered during that time was nothing short of exhilarating.

I remember my first Monday with Julie, a gentle but sharp woman with round glasses that sat too low on her nose. Her lectures on educational theory were dense, peppered with references I had never heard of before – Dewey, Freire, Montessori – names that echoed through the room like old friends I had not yet met. Julie spoke slowly, deliberately, as though she knew someone in the room needed that extra moment to process what she was saying. That someone was me.

By the second week, I had begun to understand the course structure. Each subject had its own rhythm: Irma's Tuesday tutorials were more informal, encouraging debate and exploration; Rolf's Wednesday classes had a stricter, more methodological tone, but he rewarded curiosity. Thursdays, though, were the day I looked forward to the most – not because I had four classes back-to-back, but because they were with Gunther.

Gunther was a tall man in his late forties with unruly hair and a tweed jacket that looked like it had survived many European winters. His voice was deep and slow, almost monotonous, but what he lacked in flair, he made up for in attentiveness. It was in Gunther's class that I first felt seen, not just as a student, but as a thinker. He would pause and ask, 'Sahal, what do you make of this?' as though my perspective might reveal a new truth. The confidence he extended to me planted something firm in the soil of my uncertainty.

The teaching methods confused me at first. There were no blackboards filled with notes to copy or memorisation tasks. Instead, I was expected to read pages of theory, reflect critically, and construct arguments. It felt chaotic. I would sometimes re-read a single paragraph four or five times before daring to underline anything. Slowly, painfully, however, I began to adjust. I took longer in the library, asked more questions in tutorials, and began writing drafts weeks in advance. My first assignment came back with a modest B+, of which I was so proud, with Gunther's handwritten note in the margin: *'Thoughtful and original – keep pushing!'* I pinned that paper above my bed like a badge of honour.

My classmates, although they differed from me in culture and background, gradually became familiar faces. I often sat next to Milena from Bulgaria, whose family ran a small school in her hometown. She spoke passionately about pedagogy, and although her English was not perfect, her ideas were rich. Then there was Joaquin from Argentina, who had a mischievous sense of humour and a deep interest in critical education theory. We shared a love for Paulo Freire's *Pedagogy of the Oppressed*, although we approached it from different lived experiences. My classmates knew little about Somalia, but they listened when I spoke, and in those small listening moments, I felt a kind of invisible dignity.

Yet, beneath the surface of my academic progress and newfound friendships ran a quiet current of worry. Letters from Dadaab were infrequent but weighed heavily on me.

My parents often wrote to me about their situation in the camp. Every word gnawed at me. I would read their letters in the morning and then sit in Gunther's class in the afternoon, trying to discuss post-modern educational theory while my heart lingered over an aching continent.

Olu remained my closest confidant. We sometimes met after class at the nearby halal café, where he introduced me to spicy döner wraps and thick Turkish tea. Olu was older and had seen the system for what it was – generous but unpredictable. He warned me gently, 'Don't let the good days fool you, brother. We are always on the edge. Enjoy the learning, but prepare for the storm.'

I began to understand what he meant. Although the course was fully funded and the dormitories were warm, around the fourth month, something inside me began to shift. I stopped participating in class discussions as much. I began missing occasional lectures, not out of laziness, but from exhaustion – the exhaustion of holding two lives within one body. I would sit in the library, books open in front of me, and find myself staring out of the window for long stretches. I prayed more and recited longer passages from the Quran, seeking clarity. My academic journey, which had begun with hope and fire, was now fogged by a quiet spiritual reckoning.

Gunther noticed the change. One Thursday, after class, he asked if I had a moment. We sat in his office, books stacked like towers on every surface.

'You're doing well, Sahal,' he said. 'But you seem ... distant. Is everything all right?'

I wanted to tell him everything: about the letters from home, about Olu's warnings, about the fear that my time here was not mine to keep. But I managed only a polite smile and said, 'Just tired, sir. It's been a long few weeks.' He nodded slowly, as though he knew there was more but would not press.

By the end of the fifth month, my decision was made. I would not continue with the course. I would seek asylum.

It was not a failure, but a necessity. My education had not ended, just paused. What I had gained in those months was not just academic knowledge, but a belief in my ability to think, to adapt, to matter. And perhaps, one day, in a different time and space, I would return to the classroom, not just as a student, but as someone whole again.

Asylum Over Ambition:
The Sacrifice and Hard Choices

On the day I decided to drop out of the course, I did something I had not done in weeks – I asked Olu to come to my room.

By then, Olu had become more than a friend. He was my big brother, in voice, in presence, in the way he moved through the world with that wary boldness that only a man who has lived too long on the margins could wear. We still disagreed on many things – especially his sweeping opinions about Germans, whom he referred to, without hesitation or apology, as 'white bastards'.

I had challenged him on this more than once. 'Not all of them, Olu,' I would argue. 'Gunther's helped me more than any Somali teacher ever did.'

But he would only shrug, his tone flat. 'Exceptions don't change the rule, brother.' Despite our ideological collisions, Olu was the one I turned to when the world inside me grew too heavy to hold.

That Sunday morning, sunlight spilled through the small square window above my desk as I waited for him to arrive. I had written and torn up two versions of my explanation – one focused on practicalities, the other on emotions. In the end, I said neither. When he entered, I simply told him the truth.

'My parents ... they don't want me to go back to Kenya. Things are bad in Somalia. My Father's not well. My mother says it's not safe. I can't finish the course, Olu. I have to seek asylum.'

He listened quietly; his face unreadable. For a moment, I feared I had disappointed him. Then he leant forward, arms resting on his knees.

'I did the same thing,' he said.

He told me how he had come on a three-year scholarship; how, with the help of a lawyer, the authorities had allowed him to continue studying while his asylum claim was processed. A year later, his claim was refused – they said his country, though poor, was not at war, but still, they let him stay.

'You,' he said, pointing at me with a short laugh, 'have a better chance than I ever did. Somalia is not even a functioning country. They can't send you back to rubble.' He paused; then came the warning. 'But your course ... it's only a year. They might kick you out, Sahal. If your legal status changes, they don't have to keep you.' He looked at me then, not with fear, but with the calm resolve of someone who had already walked this path.

I nodded; I had expected this. What surprised me was how light I felt after saying it aloud.

He left me with one final piece of advice: 'Don't tell your tutor, not yet. Let the lawyer do his job first.'

But I could not follow that advice. I had a few anchors in that place, but Gunther was one. The trust I had in him was perhaps not logical, but it was real. Something about the way he looked at me during our tutorials, the way he listened, gave me hope that not everyone saw me as just another refugee.

The following week, I knocked on his office door. He was reading a thick book, his glasses halfway down his nose as always.

'Sahal,' he said, smiling. 'What brings you here? Not course work, I hope – you've already submitted your assignment early.'

I sat down and took a breath.

'I have to leave the course.'

His smile vanished. He leant forward slightly, concerned. 'Is everything all right?'

'No. Not really,' I replied. 'My family's situation back home is getting worse. They don't want me to return to Kenya. I've decided to apply for asylum.'

There was a silence, but not a cold one. Gunther looked at me with the same steady expression he always had, thoughtful and measured.

'I see,' he said after a while. 'I'm sorry, Sahal, but I understand.'

He told me he knew an immigration lawyer, Martin, a semi-retired man whose firm had supported many African asylum seekers over the years. He said he would speak to the institute on my behalf, try to explain the situation, and see whether they could make an exception and let me continue my studies while the case was processed.

'I can't guarantee anything,' he said gently. 'Other students … their cases were refused. But we'll try.'

I left his office feeling lighter, almost triumphant. For the first time in weeks, the road ahead did not seem entirely dark. With Martin's help, maybe I could finish what I had started. The letter came three weeks later: a thick white envelope, plain font, the institute's seal in the top corner.

My hands shook as I opened it.

The message was cold and short: *Your enrolment has been terminated. You are to vacate the student accommodation within two weeks. No appeal will be considered.*

I stared at the words until they blurred.

Two weeks.

Two weeks to undo everything I had worked for; two weeks to pack up my small room and say goodbye to the place that had given me the closest thing to belonging.

It had come out of the blue: I hadn't even officially informed the institute about my decision to drop out and seek asylum. Gunther must have informed them; perhaps his desire to help me had triggered this strong and swift response from the institute. Either way, I had made my decision.

I took the letter to Martin, who had already begun drafting my asylum application. He was calm and methodical. 'We expected this,' he said. 'It's common. They're not obliged to house students without legal status.'

He made some calls, filed emergency papers, and, by the time the two weeks were up, he had found me a new place to live. It was not much – a small apartment on the edge of the city, still within walking distance of the student accommodation, but it had a bed, a table, a working heater, and, most importantly, a door that locked from the inside. It represented safety, even if only temporarily.

As I unpacked my few belongings in that new room, I felt no bitterness, just a slow, steady resolve building inside me. The road I had imagined – the clean academic journey, the neat graduation – was gone, but another road had opened, and I was still walking.

A Place to Begin Again

The news of my change in status must have spread – how exactly, I never quite knew. Perhaps Gunther, quietly and without fanfare, had informed the right people. Or maybe Martin, as part of my asylum application, made sure the agencies knew I was no longer a student and no longer had housing. It could even have been the institute itself, notifying the relevant agencies in its cold and bureaucratic way that one more foreign student had slipped through the cracks. Whoever passed the word on, the effect was swift and strangely generous.

First came a soft knock on the door. Two workers from the German Red Cross and the local refugee support agency were standing on the threshold of my barely furnished apartment. Their German was clear but rapid, and though I only caught every second word, I understood their intent: they had come to help.

They took notes as I showed them around: the leaking tap in the kitchen that hissed like an open secret, the unsteady toilet seat that rocked like a seesaw, the living room lamp that flickered like a dying star. I expected polite nods and perhaps a return visit scheduled for weeks later. Instead, they returned within 48 hours with a small army: a plumber, an electrician, a painter, and even a man from the local furniture depot.

While they worked, I was temporarily moved into a modest hotel room with crisp white sheets and a kettle that whistled gently in the quiet. I sat there in silence that first night, overwhelmed by the kindness of strangers, this sudden attention to my needs. It felt undeserved but deeply human. Without my even asking, help had come.

When I returned to my apartment two days later, it had been transformed. The walls were newly painted in soft cream, the leaking tap no longer sang its metallic song, and the toilet seat stood firm as if it belonged there. My living room glowed gently with a steady light. Best of all, a new bed had been placed in the corner, made from wood in place of the metal frame I had been sleeping on. On it lay a thick duvet, two brand-new pillows, and soft bedsheets; beside it was an armchair with arms wide enough to hold the weight of tired thoughts.

I stood in the middle of the room and breathed in the fresh paint and faint scent of new beginnings. Then, I lowered my head and whispered, *'Alhamdulillah'*. Praise be to Allah who sees us in our lowest moments and sends something soft and unexpected to hold us.

That Monday, I had another appointment with Martin to finalise my asylum paperwork. His office was even more cluttered than it had been the last time: shelves groaned under the weight of legal files, unanswered letters spilled from trays, and an ashtray told a story of stress in half-smoked cigarettes.

'Hello, Sahal,' he greeted me with a smile as I entered.

'I'm good, I can't complain. My apartment has been fixed, and now I have a home,' I replied. Before he could say anything, I added with a grin, 'And I hope you will fix my asylum too.'

He laughed softly. 'Great to hear about your apartment. I organised that, actually. I'm glad it's now a home. As for your asylum application,' he said, leaning back in his chair, 'I'll try my best.'

'Thank you, Martin. You're a kind man.'

We spent the next hour reviewing documents, signing declarations, and answering detailed questions. He asked again about my journey, my life in Somalia, the war, the scholarship and my decision to drop out. He took notes carefully, occasionally pausing to clarify something. I noticed how seriously he treated each part of my story – not as a case file, but as if it mattered. That gave me a quiet strength.

Once everything was complete, Martin leaned forward.

'I'll file the documents today. Normally, a decision comes within three months, sometimes sooner, sometimes a little longer, but in the meantime, you'll be supported. There are agencies that handle benefits for asylum seekers – food, rent, essentials. They'll contact you to arrange an interview.'

I nodded, absorbing the information like one learning to live again.

'Thank you again,' I said.

When I returned to my apartment that afternoon, the quiet felt less oppressive than before. It was no longer the silence of abandonment but of waiting – waiting with a bed to rest on, an armchair to sit in, and a roof that now felt as though it wanted me there.

I made tea and sat by the window. Outside, the streets of Frankfurt moved as they always had done, with people carrying shopping, riding bicycles, and bickering at the pelican crossing. None of them knew that something momentous had shifted in my world. I was no longer a student but not yet officially a refugee either; I was something in between – a man suspended between paperwork and prayer.

Subtly, though, something within me had changed. For the first time in months, maybe years, I felt less like a burden and more like a human being, not because of a piece of paper or legal status, but because someone had seen me and decided I deserved dignity. The working toilet, the warm bed, the painted wall – these small things whispered, *you matter.*

Later that week, a letter arrived inviting me to an interview for asylum support benefits. The German was dense and formal, but with the help of an English–German dictionary, I could recognise the key words. I called Martin, who explained what documents I should take and how to prepare for it. The wheels were turning.

Each morning began with a prayer; then I sat in my chair and read – sometimes the Quran, sometimes the German dictionary, sometimes nothing at all, just letting my thoughts wander to Baidoa, to Marka, to my parents in Kenya. I thought of Hindiyeey often. Was she safe? Alive? Married? Did she remember me as I remembered her? The uncertainty was heavy, but now I had a way of carrying it.

My new life had begun not with triumph, but with a few small repairs. It had started with a broken tap, a flickering light, a man with a toolbox, and a woman with a clipboard, with someone seeing that even exiles need comfort, not just survival but softness too. And so, I waited, but I was no longer waiting in the dark.

Within a week, a man and a woman from the agency that handled benefits for asylum seekers came to visit me. They both spoke good English – perhaps not by chance, but because they dealt with many refugees like me who arrived in Germany with only fragmented English and no German. I was relieved: it made everything easier.

'Sahal, we've come to assess your needs and complete a benefit application,' they said kindly, standing in the corridor of my newly refurbished apartment.

'Ah, thank you,' I replied, stepping aside to let them in.

The process was long – more than I had imagined. We completed several lengthy forms, some requiring two or three signatures on each page. They explained each section as we went, checking that I understood and often pausing to rephrase a question in simpler terms. Although I found the paperwork tiresome, I was grateful for their patience.

When we had finished, the woman looked up from her clipboard and said, 'Your application will be processed immediately. A decision should be made soon. However, if you have any urgent needs, don't hesitate to contact us. We will do our best to help.'

That last part was not just something they said; it was real. I had already run out of money for food – my scholarship bursary had been cut off two weeks earlier when I left the institute – so they handed me a stack of food vouchers. I could use these at the supermarket down the road to buy enough bread, rice, milk, lentils, fruit, and vegetables for a week – anything except clothes. I thanked them repeatedly, standing by the door as they left, holding the vouchers in my hand like scraps of hope.

Exactly two days later, a letter arrived. I found it in my letterbox: on thin paper, folded precisely in two, and written in plain German. I only grasped a few words at first, but I knew it was important. I took it to the table, placed it under the light, and began to decipher it with the help of my little German–English dictionary and what I'd learnt from Gunther's books.

The letter informed me that I had been awarded a monthly benefit of 300 German Marks. My rent and utility bills would also be covered, and every winter and summer, I would receive an additional 400 marks for clothing. I exhaled deeply. It was more than I had expected: not luxury, not abundance, but dignity – a lifeline.

Without wasting time, I tucked the letter into my jacket pocket and made my way to Martin's office. He looked up as I went in, surrounded as always by files and envelopes.

'I got this,' I said, unfolding the letter on his desk.

He read it quickly and nodded. 'This is good. Very good. Now you'll have some stability. At least you won't go hungry while we wait for the asylum decision.'

I nodded, grateful.

In those weeks of waiting, I settled into a gentle rhythm. On some afternoons, I would take the tram and visit Gunther, who lived about thirty minutes away. His wife Margareta always greeted me with a warm smile and offered me something to eat – a slice of cake, a bowl of soup, hot tea, or sometimes a plate of bread and cheese. Their home was full of life – music, books, the smell of something baking. Their two teenage daughters were always listening to Madonna on a radio cassette player that sat by the window. They spoke perfect English, and though we did not talk much, they were always kind to me, nodding or offering a friendly 'Hi Sahal!' as I walked through the door.

I had no washing machine at home. Although the agencies had done so much, this was not included. Without hesitation, Gunther and Margareta told me I could use theirs whenever I needed to.

'Don't let your clothes pile up,' Margareta would say. 'Come by. You are welcome any time.'

Gunther, for his part, never stopped supporting me intellectually. He would lend me books on educational theory, philosophy, economics, or, sometimes, beginner-level German books meant for foreign speakers. These were more than books: they were a way to fill the long, silent evenings in my apartment – evenings with no television, by choice, and no company save my thoughts and memories. During these quiet hours, by lamp-light, I would read slowly, write letters to my family, and sometimes just sit in stillness, reflecting on everything I had left behind and everything I was trying to build.

I also started visiting Olu again. He seemed different now – softer. He had begun dating a Cameroonian woman who had been granted refugee status the year before and now worked at a language school, teaching English. Olu always referred to her as 'my future wife', and the affection in his voice was unmistakable.

When he was not with her, he would visit me. We would sit in my apartment, talking for hours about life, about limbo, about the strange halfway world we found ourselves in. He had his way of talking – part hopeful, part cynical – but there was warmth in it too now, a shared understanding.

Although I was content, even grateful, there was an ache in my chest that never quite left me. I missed my parents deeply.

I missed Hindiyeey. It had been three weeks since I had last spoken to my family. I had called them from a public phone booth, days before I officially dropped out of the institute, and told them that I was seeking asylum. Their voices on the other end had been calm but heavy.

Calling them again was not simple. They had no phone in the refugee camp in Dadaab, so to reach them, I had to make two calls – one to arrange for them to be at the refugee agency office, and a second at the appointed time to speak to them. That required money, coordination, and patience. Letters were easier, although they took about a month to arrive, but they brought comfort when I received replies as well as when I sent them to my parents. They offered the time and space to convey my thoughts to my parents

I told myself I would wait. I would call them once I had an answer – rejection or acceptance – once I had something real to tell them. Until then, I waited, not with despair, but with determination. The silence between us was filled with love and *dua*. And that, for now, was enough.

A Tolerated Existence

As predicted by Martin, my lawyer, exactly three months and two days after I submitted my asylum application, a letter arrived through my letterbox. It was a two-page document, written entirely in German. The top half of the first page was dense with references to immigration laws and procedural articles, clauses stacked like bricks in a legal fortress. My eyes hurried over them, straining for the meaning I feared and expected. And there it was – in the middle of the page, written in stark, bureaucratic phrasing: my asylum application had been rejected.

The explanation was brief and to the point. The rejection was based on the fact that I had entered Germany via Kenya and had used a legal route to get there. Kenya, while not my homeland, was considered a 'safe third country', and this fact alone had tilted the scale against me. I felt the weight of those words press down on my chest. It was as though the letter had taken a deep breath and then exhaled disappointment directly into my soul.

But there was a second half to the news. The German state, acknowledging the dire conditions in Somalia and the impossibility of returning me there, granted me what they called 'Duldung' – tolerated status. With this status, I would receive the benefits offered to asylum seekers: 500 German marks per month, my rent covered, and health insurance, including dental care. Furthermore, I would be allowed to

attend a language school to study German and, in six months'
time, I would have the right to work legally.

Despite this relatively generous list of rights and allowances,
I did not feel hopeful. The word 'tolerated' itself left a bitter
aftertaste: I was not wanted, merely endured. I was a guest
who could not be sent away but who would never be invited
to stay.

I did not trust my basic German to fully understand the
document, so I folded the letter carefully and set off to see
Martin. When I arrived at his office, the receptionist – his
teenage daughter – greeted me with a polite smile. 'He's at
lunch,' she said. 'But he'll be back shortly if you'd like to
wait.'

I nodded and took a seat. The office smelled faintly of old
paper and strong coffee. I watched the receptionist quietly
typing, wondering if she knew how many lives passed
through her Father's office, teetering on the edge of legality
and hope.

Martin returned after half an hour, with a thick file under
his arm. He spotted me immediately. 'Hi Sahal, how are you?'
he asked with his usual warm but direct tone.

'I'm fine, Martin, but I've received some bad news,' I
blurted out.

'I know,' he replied calmly, 'I received a copy of the decision
this morning. Let's talk in my office.'

I followed him in and sat in the familiar chair beside his
wide, cluttered desk. Martin pulled out the letter from his own
folder and read through it again with measured eyes. One of
the many things I admired about Martin was his calmness,
almost stoic in its consistency. Nothing seemed to shake him.
He did not react with surprise or disappointment; instead, he
focused on the practical steps forward.

'This is not an unusual outcome,' he said finally, looking
up, 'The German government has rejected many cases like
yours lately. I don't know why. You have a genuine case, but
the system is shifting.'

I nodded slowly, the rejection still stinging despite his even tone. I felt myself shrinking inward, devastated, displaced, as if I had just been told by an entire country that I did not belong.

Martin continued, 'You have two options. First, you can appeal, but let me be honest: the chances of success are slim. I had a client recently who appealed and was rejected again. The second option is to accept the tolerated status, stay quiet, study the language, work hard, and in six months, you'll be allowed to work legally. From there, you build your case slowly.'

I looked at him, my voice cracking under the weight of disappointment. 'What do you think I should do?'

Martin did not hesitate. 'Don't appeal. It's a waste of time and emotional energy. Focus on moving forward. You're not being deported. You have a foothold. Use it.'

I sat back, trying to process his advice. The future I had imagined for myself felt blurry and fragile, but Martin's composure had a grounding effect on me. He did not speak in terms of hopes or dreams but of plans, strategies, and steps. Even as he delivered hard truths, he offered a way forward.

'Can I think about it and come back to you?' I asked, trying to buy time to gather myself.

'Of course. Don't rush,' he said. 'We have time. Their decision won't change tomorrow. Just let me know.'

I thanked him, shook his hand, and walked out into the afternoon. A warm April breeze touched my face as I boarded the tram home. Oddly, I was not angry. Perhaps Martin's calmness had rubbed off on me, or perhaps I had already known deep inside that this would be the outcome. I found myself thinking not of rejection but of the phrase *tolerated status*. It sounded harsh, but it was still a shelter of sorts. Perhaps, I told myself, Germany was never meant to be the final destination. Perhaps Allah had another path for me, one I could not yet see.

When I arrived at my apartment, the sun was still out. The day was unusually bright. I made a cup of tea, spread out my prayer mat, and prayed *Asr*. After the prayer, I sat quietly and said a long *dua*. I thanked Allah for my shelter, my health, and my small blessings. I asked for a way forward, for strength, for clarity.

I lay down for a nap and fell into a deep sleep. When I woke up, it was 7.30 in the evening. I had missed my *Maghrib* prayer, a rare occurrence that left me feeling guilty. I performed *wudu* quickly, prayed *Maghrib*, and then made a simple soup for dinner. I sat on the edge of my bed with the bowl in my hand, my mind turning over the contents of the letter again and again.

Rejection. Toleration. A path forward. It was not what I had hoped for, but it was not the end either, just a different kind of beginning.

I woke up early the next morning, the weight of the previous day's decision still resting on my chest like a stone, yet something in me had shifted. I felt lighter. Maybe it was sleep, maybe it was the *dua* I had made, or maybe, just maybe, it was acceptance. I had been bruised, without doubt, but I was not broken. My spirit, surprisingly, was high.

Before I had gone to bed the night before, I had sat quietly with my thoughts. Not all was lost. In fact, if I were honest with myself, there were many small blessings – subtle signs of mercy scattered throughout my life. I was in a safe country, far from Mogadishu's gunfire and the suffocating dust of Dadaab. Here, in this land of cold, order, and punctual trams, even a failed asylum seeker like me was not left to rot. I had rights, limited but real. I had a roof over my head, money, food to eat, health insurance, even dental care, which still amazed me. I was allowed to attend language school, and in six months, if nothing else changed, I could work. That mattered. It gave me hope.

And I was not alone. I had Martin, a lawyer who treated me not as a case file, but as a person. I had Gunther, who showed me what kindness looked like from a man who had no reason to care. I had Olu, my big 'brother' in exile, who always knew the right words at the right time. I was, in a strange way, surrounded by a quiet form of love, and I was grateful.

I made myself breakfast – just bread, eggs, and a strong cup of tea – and stood under the hot shower for a few minutes, letting the steam melt away the remnants of yesterday's fear. Then, dressed in my warm jacket and scarf, I prepared to leave for Martin's office. I had made up my mind: I would not appeal. I would accept the situation and move forward, however slow or uncertain that path might be. I would surrender it all to Allah and let His plan unfold.

I also decided that it was time to call my parents. I needed to let them know what had happened. They would worry, of course, but I wanted them to understand that I was safe and that, eventually, I could work and perhaps help move them from Dadaab to Garissa – a dream they had held onto for years.

Just as I was locking my apartment door, a familiar voice called out behind me.

'Morning, Sahal!'

I turned around to find Gunther and Olu standing at the bottom of the stairs, smiling. I blinked, surprised. 'Oh! What a surprise – the two of you! Good morning!'

'You weren't expecting us, yeah?' Olu grinned, his deep laugh already escaping before I could answer.

'No, not really,' I admitted, stepping outside and closing the door behind me.

Gunther spoke up, 'We were visiting an old friend nearby who hasn't been feeling well. We thought we'd drop by and say hello.'

I smiled. 'That's very kind of you. Thank you.'

'Where are you off to so early?' Gunther asked, curiosity showing on his face.

I hesitated for a second. 'I'm going to see Martin ... my lawyer.'

Olu's tone changed instantly. 'Ah. Did you hear back about your application?'

I paused again, debating how much to say, but opted for the truth. 'Yes. I got the decision yesterday. It's ... not good news. Rejected.'

'Oh no, brother. I'm so sorry to hear that,' they both said, almost in unison.

'Never mind,' I said, trying to keep my voice light. 'Maybe Germany doesn't like me.'

'Don't say that!' Gunther replied firmly. 'We love you, and we want you here. But the government ... sometimes they are too harsh.'

I checked my watch. 'Listen, I've got to go. Martin is expecting me, but let's catch up this weekend.'

We exchanged quick goodbyes, and I headed for the tram. As I sat staring out of the window, my confidence started to falter. Doubt crept in. Maybe I had been too quick to accept Martin's advice. What if this were my only chance? What if the next government changed the rules again? What if I appealed and, against all odds, won? Had I given up too soon?

I silently whispered a prayer. 'Ya Allah, give me clarity. If this decision is good for me, keep it firm in my heart. If not, open another door.'

Martin greeted me with a nod as I walked into his office.

'Good morning, Sahal.'

'Morning, Martin. I'm well, thank you.'

'I have another client in twenty minutes, so I'll be direct. Have you decided?'

'Yes,' I said, steady this time. 'I've decided not to appeal.'

He nodded. 'Good. Then I'll file the response stating that. No appeal. It's done. If anything changes – if there's a shift in policy – I'll let you know. But for now, this is the end of the road for the initial application.'

'Thank you, Martin, for everything,' I said sincerely.

'My pleasure, and keep in touch,' he replied with a gentle smile.

As I left Martin's office, I felt no certainty about the future, but I felt no fear either. That was something. That was enough for now.

On my way home, I stopped at the supermarket and bought rice, tomatoes, onions, eggs, and a packet of black tea. Carrying two heavy plastic bags, I finally reached my apartment and collapsed onto the bed, still wearing my shoes. Now my thoughts turned to my parents. How would I explain all this to them? They did not know the bureaucracy of Europe. The term 'rejected but not deported' would confuse them. How could I tell them that the door was closed but not locked, that I had no answers but still carried hope?

Later that afternoon, I walked to the post office and tried to call the UN office to schedule a call with my Father. It was closed. I returned the next day, and a kind Kenyan lady helped arrange the call.

'You can call back this afternoon,' she said jovially.

When the call connected, my heart raced. 'Hello, hello, salaamu alaikum Aabo, can you hear me?'

A few seconds passed before his voice came clearly down the line, in his familiar Maay-Maay accent.

'Haa ki dheegoow, alankeey. Yes, I can hear you, son.'

I explained everything: my rejection, my tolerated status, my decision not to appeal. I expected disappointment, even panic, but they were calm, so calm.

'We'll keep making *dua*,' my mother said. 'Allah has a better plan.'

The call ended with warmth, blessings, and renewed hope. I paid and walked home with something I had not felt in days: relief, as if a heavy weight had lifted.

A Future Once Imagined Now Reimagined

The days that followed my asylum rejection were turbulent, like sailing in a small boat across stormy seas with no anchor, no compass, and no clear shore in sight. Some days, I woke up with nothing weighing on me, full of motivation, determined to redesign my future. On other days, the memory of the decision, the coldness of it, the finality, returned like an unfamiliar shadow. It suffocated me. I could not shake off the feeling that the version of life I had once dreamt of – secure, dignified, full of possibilities – was gone. The rejection had wiped the slate clean, not in a hopeful, fresh-start sort of way, but more like an erasure, the disappearance of all I had mentally and emotionally built up over the years.

I was not alone, however. Olu and Gunther became, in their unique ways, steady beams in my unstable architecture. Olu, pragmatic and always in the now, reminded me that we were in the same boat – undocumented but breathing. He had plans to marry his Cameroonian fiancée and was already dreaming aloud about starting a business in a few years. 'You can't live inside a decision letter,' he told me once over tea. 'You read it, you fold it, you file it away, and then you live. Live for something in the future, don't dwell on the past.'

Gunther, ever the optimist, was more philosophical. 'Sahal, even without refugee papers, you have protection, healthcare, food, housing, and you're in school. That's something.' He spoke slowly and thoughtfully, choosing each English word as if it were a chess piece. 'Don't forget, this country respects rules. Even if it's not perfect, you are not invisible here.'

They both made sense. Their perspectives certainly gave me comfort but at the same time, neither walked in my shoes. They could not feel the blisters or the pain beneath the surface of my smile. My pain had deep roots – in memory, in history, in longing.

Hindiyeey

I had not heard her voice in three years. I did not know whether she was in Dadaab, Nairobi, or somewhere else entirely. Maybe she was married, maybe waiting. But I knew one thing: if she had any idea where I was, she would have hoped that I would succeed – that I would make it here, get the papers, and start a new life. She would have imagined our reunion: a future stitched together after war had torn us apart, a home somewhere in Germany or beyond, maybe children, maybe stability. That imagined future was now broken, scattered across my thoughts like shattered glass.

And my parents – two old souls trapped in the limbo of Dadaab – had pinned all their remaining hope on me. I was their exit plan, their opportunity for retirement, their chance to live once again as people, not numbers in a refugee registry. Now, with no legal status, I felt that I had failed them too. My rejection did not just close a door; it collapsed a whole building that I had spent years constructing in my mind.

And yet, as they say, time is the greatest healer. Two months after my rejection, something unexpected happened: I began to feel alive again, slowly, quietly, almost without noticing it. It started with the language. I had been going to my integration course more consistently and, with Gunther's help, had enrolled in a reputable language school that served both asylum seekers and those already granted refugee status. The classes were rigorous but human. The teachers spoke slowly, smiled often, and corrected us gently. I could now buy food at the bakery with confidence, ask directions without panicking, and even laugh at some of the local jokes, although German humour still puzzled me at times.

Outside the classroom, I built a new routine. I joined the public library not far from my apartment. It was a quiet, sunlit space, always clean and stocked with endless knowledge. The first book I borrowed was about German history, the second a slim volume on educational philosophy. By the fourth week, I had a backpack full of titles: philosophy, science, sociology, even theology. Reading became my new escape, my new prayer. I studied not just to pass the time, but to rebuild the person I thought I had lost.

And then, something beautiful happened. I went back to the reading list from the teacher-training course I had dropped out of and re-read the work of those names once alien to me: Dewey, Vygotsky, Bruner, and Bloom. I read not to pass exams, because there were none, but with a new sense of purpose. Their theories made sense: the ideas that learning is social, that knowledge is constructed, that potential is not fixed – these spoke to me, soothed me, made me believe again in my capacity to grow.

Financially, things were not easy, but I managed. Out of the small monthly benefit I received, I saved a little and sent it to my parents every month. My Father always sent back a letter of thanks, handwritten in Maay-Maay, and sealed with love. He ended every letter in the same way: 'Beesadii bisha ha qaadani – We received the monthly remittance.' Those few words became my quiet anthem, my reason to keep going.

Knowing that I could still be useful – even as a rejected asylum seeker – changed something fundamental in me. I no longer measured my value by a legal stamp on a piece of paper. I measured it by what I gave, what I learned, and how I grew. My status had not changed, but my state of mind had. I was no longer waiting for Germany to accept me. I was building a life, however uncertain, within the limits that existed.

'A Future Once Imagined Now Reimagined.' That was the new script I lived by. The old future – a safe job, papers, a house, and maybe Hindiyeey by my side – all disappeared, but a new future was slowly taking shape, one where I was a student of life, a worthy son, a man who had fallen but refused to disappear. The rejection did not define me; it redefined me, and in that painful, humbling transformation, I began to see glimpses of the man I might still become.

I continued to read widely while awaiting my work permit. The library had become both a sanctuary and a silent tutor: its high shelves, dusty volumes, and quiet corners offered me a daily reminder that the mind could still grow even when the body remained in limbo. Frankfurt, with its strange and accidental hospitality, allowed me to explore a side of myself that I had not known existed. I was absorbing knowledge not just to pass time but to prepare myself for the life I was still determined to live.

The city, too, slowly opened up, like a book I was only beginning to understand. I explored its streets, observed its people, wandered into its art galleries, and frequented Turkish cafeterias where the scent of strong tea, cardamom, and fresh simit lingered in the air and evoked memories. These modest walks and simple drinks became rituals. I would sit with a small notebook, scribbling reflections or reading a book I had borrowed from the library, writing down ideas about justice, identity, education, or sometimes just a poem I tried to translate into German for practice.

My parents remained a strong source of emotional grounding. Each month, I sent money to the refugee camp in Kenya, where they were still awaiting a miracle. Their gratitude, their prayers, and their belief in me gave me a sense of purpose. My Father continued to write to me, his letters arriving late but always bringing light. His familiar closing line, 'Beesadii bisha ha qaadani – We received the monthly remittance' made me feel not just like a son, but like a lifeline. Despite my 'tolerated' status, despite the rejection stamped on my papers, I mattered to someone. To them, I was more than my legal status – I was their hope.

Gunther and his family were now like extended family to me. I visited them often, and they received me warmly each time. His children would run to greet me, and his wife always insisted I stay for dinner. Gunther remained unshakably optimistic about my case, offering a mix of legal explanation and personal encouragement that I had come to appreciate more than I admitted.

Frankfurt, in every technical and legal sense, had rejected me: I was not welcome in terms that mattered to bureaucrats or politicians. I was not a Frankfurter. I did not have the papers, the passport, or the promise. But emotionally, intellectually, spiritually – I was here, living, growing, contributing. I was reading their books, drinking their tea, walking their streets, and learning their language. I paid for my tram ticket, sorted my waste into the right bins, and smiled at strangers when our eyes met on Sunday mornings. I was here; although uninvited, I was still here.

One evening, as I sat in my room reading *The Clown* by Heinrich Böll, I heard a loud knock at my door. It was unexpected and strangely forceful. My first instinct was one of suspicion. Gunther was away with his family on a short trip to Bonn, and Olu always called before visiting. I was not expecting anyone. I stood silently for a moment, then peered through the peephole.

It was Olu.

I opened the door. 'Hello, Olu, is everything all right?' I asked, my voice rising with surprise.

'Yes and no, brother,' he replied in a serious tone. 'Can I come in?'

'Of course, come on in,' I said, stepping aside.

He sat in my armchair, his shoulders slouched and his face tired. Something was not right. I offered him tea, but he declined with a wave of his hand.

'I have something to tell you, brother,' he began. 'You know I was planning to marry Eve, my Cameroonian fiancée?'

'Yes,' I said, interrupting him, 'you talked about a December wedding.'

'Well,' he paused, 'the wedding is now off.'

I stared at him, unsure whether I had heard right. 'Rewind, rewind. Can you repeat that?'

'She came to me yesterday,' he said, his eyes now starting to redden, 'and told me she's calling it off. She wants to focus on her teaching career. She said she's not ready to start a family.'

I did not know what to say. I sat silently for a moment, letting his words settle in the room.

'Is there someone else?' I asked gently.

'I don't know, brother. Maybe … maybe not. I'm not sure.'

His voice trembled, and I saw tears start to form. I had only met Eve once, but she had struck me as composed and articulate, far more mature than many women of her age. I suspected there was more to this story than Olu was admitting. Was it his failed asylum application? His drinking? His lack of any long-term plan?

'I don't know Eve well,' I said cautiously, 'but do you want me to talk to her? Maybe I can find out why.'

He looked up with a faint sense of hope. 'Yes, please.'

'All right. Tomorrow is Saturday and I'm free. I'll go to her apartment, just knock on the door without telling her. Let's see what happens.'

'Sounds good, brother,' he said, finally accepting the tea I had made earlier.

After an hour of conversation that veered between heartbreak and hope, Olu left, looking slightly less burdened.

The next afternoon, after lunch, I boarded the same tram I used to take to Martin's office. Eve lived not far from there. As I approached her building, I noticed the kitchen windows were open. I could hear voices – one male, one female. I hesitated for a moment before knocking.

To my surprise, Eve herself opened the door, smiling.

'Hello, Sahal. Welcome! You've never been here before – who told you I live here?'

I smiled. 'A little bird. Are you busy?' I asked. 'I wanted to have a word with you.'

'Of course, come in. I have two friends over, but they're just leaving,' she said, leading me inside. I was surprised that she welcomed me into her house, given that I had only met her once.

She quickly introduced me to her friends; after a few minutes, they left, and we were alone. Her apartment was neat and warm. Two black leather sofas faced each other, and a small bookshelf stood in the corner. It felt like the home of someone who read and thought a lot.

'Would you like anything to drink?' she asked.

'A glass of water, please,' I replied. I took a moment before speaking. 'Eve, I apologise for coming unannounced. Maybe it was not polite, but I came to ask you something, something I think only you can answer.'

She nodded slowly, her face calm.

'You probably know why I'm here. It's about Olu. He told me the wedding is off.'

She looked down for a moment, then met my gaze. 'Yes, it's true. I broke off the engagement. It saddens me, but it had to be done.' She paused before continuing. 'We were planning a December wedding. I told my family, and even tried on a wedding dress. But the more I thought about it, the more I realised I couldn't go through with it.'

'Why?' I asked gently.

'Olu is ... friendly, charming even, but he's not serious. He has no plan. He drinks more than I'm comfortable with. He doesn't seem to think about the future in the way I need someone to. I can't build a life with a man who floats from one day to the next.'

Her words were calm but firm. It was clear this decision had not come easily, but she had made up her mind.

'I'm still friends with him,' she said, 'but there is no going back. That chapter is closed.'

I listened quietly. There was nothing I could say to change her mind. I respected her honesty, even if it hurt to hear. 'If this is what you believe is best for both of you, then I wish you peace,' I said.

She thanked me for understanding.

I left her apartment with a heavy heart. I thought of Olu and how devastated he would be when I told him. His dreams, like mine once, had collapsed – unexpectedly, suddenly, painfully. Another future imagined would now need to be reimagined.

As I walked home under the grey Frankfurt sky, I realised how fragile plans, people, and love are, but also how essential it is to face those fragilities with grace. We had all lost something – a country, our status, those we loved – but we had not yet lost ourselves.

I met Olu the following day and told him what Eve said. To my great surprise, he was philosophical and dignified about the break.

'It is what it is, brother. As she said, we are friends and that is where we are now,' he said.

'Good for you, brother, I am glad you are taking it so gracefully, and I am sure there are many more fish in the sea.'

When Gunther and his wife heard that Olu and Eve were not getting married, they were distraught because they were the ones who had introduced them to one another.

A Right to Work, A Stranger Still

I received my work permit earlier than expected, a month before the official six-month mark. It arrived in a pale brown envelope, neat and bureaucratic, the kind of letter that felt too important for its size. It simply confirmed what I had already hoped: I was now permitted to work anywhere in Germany. Anywhere – a word so wide and liberating, and yet, oddly, so hollow.

This new legal right meant that I could go beyond Frankfurt, seek work in other cities, maybe even chase better pay or opportunities, but I was not going anywhere. Frankfurt had become home, and I did not say that lightly. I had friends here – Olu and Gunther. I had a decent apartment. I knew which trams to catch, where to get Turkish tea, and which bookshops sold second-hand German grammar books. I could walk the streets without a map. That, to me, was belonging. I was not ready to exchange that for another version of displacement.

Having a right, however, is different from knowing what to do with it. So, I went to Gunther.

'How do I even begin?' I asked him one evening, as we sat on the stone steps near the Römerberg, in the heart of the old city.

Gunther listened as he always did, with patience and intent. 'You start where you are, my friend,' he said, 'There are employment agencies. I'll help you register.'

And he did. We registered with three agencies that specialised in low-skilled labour. I quickly learnt that although

I was permitted to work, the opportunities available to someone like me – someone with no formal qualifications, still learning the German language, and with an asylum application still pending were very few. The only jobs I could reasonably apply for were menial: cleaning dishes, loading warehouse pallets, filling supermarket shelves, or washing cars.

To my surprise, within a month of registering, I began to get offers, but none felt quite right. Some paid too little; others required me to travel long distances on trams or buses that would eat up my day. One required me to change trams three times, a logistical nightmare for a job that barely paid the minimum wage. Then came a small opportunity that fitted. A family-owned carpet shop needed someone to assist customers with loading the carpets they had bought into their cars. That was it, nothing fancy, nothing complicated. It was not physically demanding, and it was close to home. I took it.

The work was simple. Customers would browse and choose a carpet. Once the sale was completed, I would carry it, rolled, heavy and awkward, out to their car. Some tipped me with coins, others with kind smiles. For a while, I felt the peace of a routine, but the pay was not enough. After a month, I left, emboldened by having something new to add to my CV.

That short line of work experience on my CV unlocked another door. I found a car wash job – full-time, decently paid, but with long hours. I worked twelve-hour shifts from 7.30 a.m. to 7.30 p.m., with only short breaks. I was one of five attendants, and though the mornings were manageable, the afternoons were relentless. The cars came in one after another, and we scrubbed, sprayed, vacuumed, and polished until our hands stung. Still, I stuck with it for three solid months.

The work gave me stability. My wages covered my rent and expenses and allowed me to support my parents in Dadaab. That was no small thing. The car wash job became a bridge not just from poverty to a modest livelihood, but from helplessness to dignity. But it came at a cost: the hours left little space for anything else. My own studies suffered, and

I had little time for Gunther and Olu. By the time I arrived home, it was already dark. I cooked, ate, cleaned, and fell into bed. Weekdays disappeared in a blur of water hoses and drying cloths.

Still, there were small blessings: I finally installed a landline phone in my flat and no longer had to queue at public phone booths to call my family. I could dial my parents in Kenya from the comfort of my tiny kitchen and hear their voices without worry. That alone gave me solace.

Then something unexpected happened. Our line supervisor quit out of the blue, and the position became vacant.

'Sahal,' Alket, the branch manager, said to me one afternoon, 'you should apply.'

Alket was an Albanian Muslim, observant and deeply kind. He had respect for Black, Muslim, undocumented people like me. Despite my legal limbo, he treated me as if I mattered. He gave me time off for Friday prayers and longer breaks when I needed them to catch the *khutbah* at the nearby Turkish-run mosque. We had formed a quiet friendship rooted in mutual respect.

'I'm not sure,' I told him, hesitantly. 'Let me think about it.'

I was comfortable in my current position. I had no responsibilities beyond my shift. When work ended, so did the stress. Becoming a supervisor would mean more pay, yes, but also more pressure. I would be the first to arrive, the last to leave. I would be responsible if anything went wrong. The advantages, however, would be better pay, more time supervising than washing, and, most compelling of all, Alket promised to drive me to and from work – no more long tram rides or waiting on icy platforms. That alone felt like a blessing.

I slept on the decision. The next morning, I submitted my application. There were no other applicants. The interview was a formality rather than a genuine hurdle. Alket and the business owner – a man of Turkish heritage named Latif, who rarely interfered in daily operations – sat across from me.

They asked a few questions, and I answered honestly. I knew the work. I knew the rhythm of the place; I had established myself with key customers, and I got on well with my co-workers. I got the job.

My salary doubled; this meant I no longer qualified for social benefits, but I did not mind. After paying my bills, I had enough disposable income to move my parents out of Dadaab into Garissa, a safer, more stable place. I paid $100 each month for a two-bedroom house and covered their other living expenses. My Father and mother were overjoyed. For them, this was a new chapter. They now had a home with a roof, walls, and, perhaps most meaningfully, a phone. I could speak to them daily. My success, small as it was, gave them peace. That alone made every long day at work, washing and supervising, worth it.

Oddly, although I was now opening and closing the car wash, I found I had more time. Maybe it was the lack of commute; maybe it was the pride of earning more, or maybe it was the peace of knowing my parents were safe. Whatever it was, I felt more energised, more hopeful and, at times, I forgot I was a failed asylum seeker.

Then, one Friday, I called Olu. I had not heard from him in weeks. We were both busy with life.

'Olu, how are you, my brother?' I asked.

His voice was quieter than usual. 'Not much, my brother. Alright, I guess.'

Something in his tone unsettled me. 'Let's meet. Next Friday?'

'Sure. What time?'

'Any time from 10.00 am.'

'Okay. Let's meet at 11.00. Your place or mine?'

'My place.'

That Friday, he came. I was shocked by his appearance: he had lost weight and his eyes looked tired and sunken. The fire in him had dimmed; the light in his smile had gone.

After we had eaten, I gently asked what was going on.

'To be honest, brother,' he said, his voice trembling, 'I'm not coping well with the breakup. I feel devastated, like I lost a part of me.' He paused, then continued. 'I thought Eve was the one – my soulmate. I built everything around that belief, but I was wrong. We men plan, but women always counterplan.'

He talked, and I listened. He unburdened himself slowly and painfully. Every word was raw. I did not interrupt; I let him pour out his grief, not intending to fix it, but simply to receive it.

Then, when the moment came, I spoke.

'Olu, my brother. I hear you. And I am sorry. But sometimes, no matter how hard we try, we can't control these things. You did your part, but Eve chose differently. That's not your fault. Don't beat yourself up. Even in love, you have agency; you must move on. You always said, 'Forget the past and live for the future and its endless possibilities.'

He nodded. His eyes softened.

'Thank you, brother. I'm trying. But it takes time.'

'I understand,' I said. 'Tea?'

'Yes, please.'

After he left, I began my preparations for Friday prayer – an important practice in my week, a ritual I had promised myself that I would never miss.

In the months that followed, life continued – work, prayers, conversations with Olu and Gunther, calls to my parents. I was still an asylum seeker, a failed one, and still without papers, but I had a job, a phone line, and a sense of purpose, however fragile. And that mattered, because even though I remained a stranger in the eyes of the state, I was no longer a stranger to myself.

Part IV – Reunion

The Call That Brought the Rain

The cold was stubborn that December morning – a bitter sort of cold, not the kind that bites and fades, but the kind that sits in your bones, slows you down, and makes you linger a little longer under the covers even when the alarm goes off.

It had been a long week. Frankfurt was heaving with shoppers: the festive season always brought out crowds in droves. People seemed eager to clean not just their homes but their cars too, as if a spotless vehicle could help them steer more cleanly into the new year. At the car wash, this meant hours of scraping off thick layers of grime: snow turned to slush, turned to black ice. Every car that pulled in looked as though it had driven through a battlefield. My arms were sore from wielding the pressure hose, and the smell of detergent had found its way into my skin.

So that Saturday, I did nothing. I had earned my idleness. The plan was simple: to stretch the morning out, maybe get to the library by noon if the weather stayed kind, and treat myself to a Turkish kebab on the walk there. The thought of grilled meat wrapped in warm flatbread, steam rising into the crisp air, made me momentarily forget my aching shoulders.

The phone rang twice, then died. That was odd. Five minutes later, it rang again, this time more insistently. I looked at the screen: there was no name, just numbers – a long string of them, so it was an international call. My first thought was of my parents, but they never called on Saturdays. They knew

I worked long hours during the week; Sundays were our time. Still, I picked up.

'Hello?'

There was a pause. Then a voice, faint, almost testing itself against the line. 'Sahal?'

'Yes,' I replied, unsure. Something stirred, something from a long time ago.

'It's Nuunoow. Do you remember me?'

The name tugged at a closed door in my mind. Then it creaked open. 'Nuunoow ... Guduudoow's older brother? From primary school?'

'Yes!' He laughed, relieved. 'Walaal, how are you?'

'Nuunoow! Subhanallah. I remember you now! How could I forget? How are you, brother?'

My heart, quiet moments ago, began to pace.

He had been much older than me, already on his way to adulthood when I was still at primary school, but his younger brother, Guduudoow, had been in my class. He was quiet and studious and had a mild limp from a bout of childhood polio. He used to speak of Nuunoow as if he were a prince studying in a far-off kingdom. 'One day, he will come back,' he would say, 'and work for the Ministry of Agriculture.'

But the ministry, like the nation, had collapsed into ash and memory.

'I've been in the Netherlands all this time,' Nuunoow said. 'Finished my studies. Got married to a Dutch woman. We have two boys now. Life went on.'

He spoke gently about the ones who hadn't made it. His Father, Kuukaay, the Quran teacher who sat under the big tree near our old school, had passed away; two siblings too. Guduudoow, their frail mother, and his two sisters were now in Garissa.

'I got your number from Guduudoow,' he said. 'He visited your parents and told me to call you. There's... good news.'

I straightened up. 'Good news?'

A silence fell. Then he asked, 'Do you remember Hindiyeey?'

My heart skipped two beats. The world spun, then slowed. My chest tightened. Thoughts crashed into one another like waves in a storm: *Is she dead? Did she marry someone else? Is she in Europe? Dead or married, how could either be good news?*

I did not realise that I had not answered until he said, 'Are you still there, Sahal?'

'Yes, yes. I'm here,' I said, almost choking on my voice.

He continued, his voice a little more certain now, 'Her family made it to Finland, sponsored from Ethiopia. They've been there a few months.'

Everything around me fell away.

'She's still in Addis,' he went on. 'She was left behind to start with, but they say she's joining them in the next few months.' Then came the part that stopped my heart: 'The cousin marriage didn't happen. It collapsed. Her Father refused to force it.' I leant forward, placing a trembling hand on the desk, the phone cradled against my ear. I needed to steady myself. My legs had betrayed me.

'You're serious?' I whispered.

'Walaahi,' really he said, 'I spoke to her family. They gave me her number in Addis. She does not know I have your number … but I had to tell you.' He paused, then asked gently, 'Do you want it?'

I could not speak; I just nodded.

He read the number slowly, and I scribbled it down with a pen that barely worked in my trembling fingers. That slip of paper felt like a map drawn on holy parchment, a path back to something I'd buried long ago beneath years of silence, exile, and unspoken grief.

'Mahadsanid, walaal,' thank you brother I whispered. 'I don't know what to say.'

'Then don't,' he said kindly. 'Just … call her.'

And just like that, the line went dead, but something in me came alive.

There are moments in a man's life when the past rises up, like steam from a cracked street after heavy rainfall. That call brought the rain, not the kind that drenches your coat or muddies your shoes, but the kind that soaks deep into memory and draws up everything you thought you had laid to rest.

I sat in the silence of my room, the winter light slanting across the floor. Outside, a crow cawed – an omen, or a witness, I was not sure. The scrap of paper lay before me like a summons, the numbers on the scrap paper magnified. In the air, I could feel that something was about to change: not just a reunion, not just an old love found again. Something far more profound awaited me – the reawakening of a part of myself I had long abandoned, a voice I had silenced, a tenderness I had hidden away to survive the long winters of displacement.

I looked at the number once more. I was not ready, but I was going to call.

I looked at the number again, thinking how in the next few minutes, I would be speaking to Hindiyeey, after three years of life lived in the unknown. I dialled the number; it rang once, twice … Then a woman's voice came down the crackly line.

'*Man new?*' she said, in Amharic. 'Who is this?'

I swallowed hard. My mouth had gone dry.

'Erm… erm… can I speak to Hindiyeey, please?' I said, barely recognising my own voice. I sounded like a boy again – uncertain, trembling.

There was a pause.

Then, in crisp English, she replied, 'Sure. Hold on a minute.'

I exhaled.

But then came a quick follow-up: 'Can I ask who is calling?'

'It's … it's Sahal. Her friend, from Germany,' I blurted out, quickly and awkwardly, fearing the moment might vanish like smoke.

'Germany?' she echoed, curiosity rising in her voice. 'Okay. Hold on.'

And then there was silence, not a true silence, but the kind where your heart beats so loudly in your chest that it drowns out the world. My palms were sweating; I gripped the receiver with both hands. The seconds stretched out, heavy and endless. I was not breathing – I could not. This was not classic fear, but a mixture of emotion and an anticipation of the unknown.

Then, from so far away, across borders and wounds, I heard her.

'Hello? Sahal?'

What followed was not just a cry – it was the kind of cry that breaks something open inside you, a cry filled with joy.

'Hindiyeey? Is that you?'

More sobs. I pressed the phone tighter to my ear, holding back tears of my own.

'Please don't cry ... please, don't cry,' I begged gently, almost whispering. 'All praise is due to Allah, the Lord of the Worlds. This, this is a moment I never thought would come.'

But she could not stop; through her sobs, she kept saying my name, over and over again, 'Sahal ... Sahal ... Sahal ...', each repetition like a thread stitching our broken story back together.

After ten minutes of sobbing and repeating my name, Hindiyeey regained her composure. 'I thank God for uniting two souls – only He knows how deeply they missed each other,' she said.

She told me that two days ago, she had heard from a neighbour in Addis Ababa that my parents were in Garissa and that I was in Europe, although the neighbour was not sure exactly where. She said that she had been determined to find my parents' telephone number in order to learn more about me. She explained that in two months, she would be joining her family in Finland, and that it was true that the planned marriage to her cousin had collapsed: she had refused to marry him, and her Father did not want to force her. She told me how they had initially fled to Djibouti and, after two years there, moved on to Ethiopia.

I told her about everything I had been through, my situation in Germany, how happy I was to hear her voice, and how much I had missed her. After half an hour, I told her that I would call her back the next afternoon.

After I hung up, the enormity of what had just happened began to sink in. I could not believe that I had spoken to Hindiyeey, that she was safe, and about to travel to Europe with guaranteed papers. Her voice had not changed, and, above all, the arranged marriage, which had felt like the death of our planned future together, had failed to materialise. I kept thanking God for making this impossible scenario possible.

Over the next two months, we continued to call each other at least twice a week. My life completely changed for the better; even my parents noticed how much happier I was. After keeping the news to myself for a while, I finally told them that I had reconnected with Hindiyeey.

My mother had been aware of our relationship, but my Father had always been old-fashioned when it came to loving a girl. He believed that real love was arranged by parents: you see a girl you like, you talk to her family, and they give her to you in marriage. That was his ideal model of a good and lasting relationship.

I kept dreaming about Hindiyeey, of building a home with her, starting a family, living together as a married couple. I did not know where this would happen, but I was sure it would.

A week before her flight, she told me that she intended not to live with her family in Finland, but to come to me in Germany. While I was delighted to hear this, I did not want to be selfish. I wanted her to take her time, get her papers, and come to Germany on her own terms. I also told her that, although I was working and felt to some degree content, my asylum had been rejected, and I did not see Germany as my future. I would not want to raise a family under the shadow of a failed asylum claim.

'Sahal, I know my family,' she said suddenly. 'They may organise another arranged marriage. I can't risk this again.'

'I understand,' I replied. 'But remember, no one can force you in Finland. The legal system is different.'

'But my Father and mother will still try,' she said. 'They still expect me to obey them, no matter what the law of the land is.'

I was in a dilemma: I wanted Hindiyeey to get her papers – I did not want her to live in the shadows as I did – but at the same time, I desperately wanted her to be with me. Hindiyeey, however, seemed to have made up her mind.

A Ticket to Finland,
but a Heart Set on Germany

The day came. Hindiyeey boarded her flight from Addis Ababa's international airport to Helsinki. Like me, this was her first journey to Europe, and, like me, she did not speak the language of her destination. Her path, though, differed from mine when I left for Germany nearly two years earlier. I had left with the official intention of completing my teaching course and returning to Kenya, but deep down, I had known I was not returning. I had wanted to escape from the horrors of civil war and the economic destitution of the refugee camps. I had carried with me a suitcase of uncertainty and a pocket of unknown dreams. She, however, was flying with certainty stamped on her ticket – she had an approved asylum claim, guaranteed papers upon arrival, and full refugee rights granted before even setting foot on Finnish soil.

Her flight was not a gamble like mine; it was no leap into the unknown, but a one-way promise – there would be no return ticket. Finland had opened its doors, but she knew in her heart that it was not her final destination. She was not heading to Finland to settle there, but as a formality. Her real destination – the one her soul was pointing to – was Germany, me, Sahal.

We spoke on the phone before she left for the airport. Her voice was calm but carried real conviction. 'I'm transiting through Amsterdam,' she said. 'Just a few hours stopover, then straight to Finland.'

I made *dua* for her. 'May Allah protect your journey and guide you every step of the way. Call me as soon as you land in Helsinki. I'll be waiting.'

'I will. I love you, Sahal,' she said softly.

I whispered back, 'I love you too.' Then she was gone, soaring through the skies, moving towards a new chapter – still uncertain, but with purpose in her heart.

Two days passed, and I heard nothing, but I was not worried. I imagined her settling in, finding her feet, surrounded by her family in a strange new land where snow blanketed the streets and the language curled like frost in the air. I trusted that she was safe, that she had made it, and I knew it was only a matter of time before she called me.

The call came on the third day, just as I returned from work.

'Sahal, my love, it's Hindiyeey. I'm in Helsinki. I'm sorry I didn't call sooner … I'm new here and didn't know how to reach you. I didn't want to use the family phone … I didn't want them to know who I was calling.'

My chest loosened. 'I understand, my love. Not to worry. I'm just glad you've arrived safely. How is everyone at home?'

'They're all good, my love,' she said, 'but I'm running out of coins. I'm using a public phone booth. I'll call you tomorrow.'

'Okay, speak to you soon,' I said.

The line went dead, but her words lingered. She was in Finland, but I knew that her heart and mind were already with me in Germany.

Over the next three months, while Hindiyeey settled into her new life in Finland, we continued to call each other almost every day. After work, I always looked forward to coming home, knowing I would be speaking to her on the phone. Our conversations had become the most cherished part of my daily routine; each call evoked memories of happier times in Marka and Baidoa.

At work, my responsibilities had changed: I was no longer washing cars but instead supervising others. This new role brought with it a sense of dignity and, more importantly, it left me with more energy. I was not coming home exhausted any longer, and now had the energy to read, think, and reflect. My evenings were calmer, and my weekends more social. I began going out more often, usually to meet Gunther and Olu for coffee, and sometimes for dinner on Saturday evenings.

One evening, over tea at our usual spot, I told Gunther that Hindiyeey, my childhood sweetheart, was now in Finland and was considering joining me in Germany. He was genuinely happy for me and said it was a blessing that she was finally in Europe, much closer than when she was back in Africa. Then, however, with the care of a true friend who did not want me to rush into any decision, he advised against her coming to Germany too soon. He felt it would be wiser for her to stay in Finland, apply for her papers, and wait until she had official residency before thinking of relocating.

Gunther was not alone in this opinion. Martin, my lawyer, with whom I had also shared the news, offered the same advice: that it would be better for our long-term future if Hindiyeey settled in Finland and I eventually joined her, even if it meant waiting for years. His words were logical and well-reasoned. My head agreed with him and with Gunther. My heart, though, longed for her to be with me in Germany, no matter what.

However, I kept my feelings in check. I did not want to pressure her; I wanted her to decide for herself what she felt was best. Yet deep down, I hoped her heart would lead her to me in Germany and unite our souls.

A Promise to Her Father

Our relationship had always been lived in the shadows of letters, whispers, and hidden meetings. Other than her younger brother, who used to meet us after school in Baidoa and in the summer holidays before we went back to Marka, no one in Hindiyeey's family knew the depth of our bond. My own family, on the other hand, and especially my mother Suleey, knew everything. She had always liked Hindiyeey, even when we were still teenagers.

Then came the phone call that would change everything. It was a quiet Sunday evening, and I answered eagerly when the phone rang. Hindiyeey's voice, calm but firm, echoed in my small apartment.

'Sahal, my love, the time has arrived. Before someone else comes to ask my Father for permission to marry me, you need to do so, and you must do it next week.'

My heart froze for a second. I had dreamt of this moment for years, but the reality of calling a man I had never met, a respected former civil servant, a Father protective of his daughter, felt overwhelming. What if he refused? What if he did not think I was good enough? Would Hindiyeey stand by me if her Father said no? Would she leave everything to be with me? If she did, what scars would it leave in her family? My Father always said that a girl who had a poor relationship with her Father would always have a poor relationship with her future husband.

But there was no more hiding: I had waited long enough, and she had waited even longer.

'Okay,' I said, steadying my voice. 'I will call your Father,' I added, feeling emboldened.

Hindiyeey's Father, Jabriil, was a Northerner who spoke with a Mahaa Tiri accent, precise and firm. He had served as a high-ranking civil servant before the civil war scattered us across continents. Although he barely knew my family, there was one link: my mother and Hindiyeey's mother were both from the Bakool region and had known each other since childhood. It was a thread I hoped he would remember.

The next morning, I asked Hindiyeey to send me her Father's number and told her I needed to inform my own family before making the call. She agreed.

First, I called my Father. He listened patiently and then gave me his blessing. My mother was delighted.

'Hindiyeey has a good family,' she said. 'That will be a worthy marriage. May Allah make it easy.'

Her words filled me with warmth. I held onto her prayers like an amulet.

The night before the call, I was unable to sleep. My mind imagined every possible outcome. What would I say? How would I introduce myself? What if he laughed, or worse, got angry? Sunday morning arrived. I said my *Fajr* prayers and sat silently, waiting. My hands were cold and trembling, but my heart was steady. Unbeknownst to me, Hindiyeey had warned her Father, without giving details, that someone important would be calling him from Germany.

Finally, I dialled the number.

'Hello, is that Hindiyeey's Father?' I asked as soon as the call went through.

'Haa, waa Jabriil. Waa kuma? Yes, this is Jabriil, who is calling?' he replied in his strong Northern accent.

'My name is Sahal Diinoow. You may not know me, but Hindiyeey and I went to the same middle school in Baidoa, and later we both went to Marka, although we studied at different high schools. My mother, Suleey, knows your family from Baidoa. My parents are now in Kenya. I'm in Germany and have been here for the last two years. Hindiyeey gave me your number. I called to speak about something important. Is now a good time?'

Surprisingly, my voice was calm. As soon as he had answered the phone, the fear I had built up vanished.

'Yes,' he said. 'I was expecting your call. Hindiyeey told me someone would be contacting me from Germany. We can talk.'

I took a deep breath and went to the heart of my call.

'I am calling to ask for your daughter's hand in marriage. I may not have legal papers at the moment, but I am a hard-working and responsible young man. I want to protect and provide for your daughter. Our relationship began back in our school days. After surviving war, separation and hardship, we believe it is Allah's will that we reunite and build a future together.'

There was a long silence. When he finally spoke, his voice was calm and wise.

'Tell me about your current situation. And your family – who is your Father?'

I answered honestly. I told him about my immigration status, my work and my plans. I explained who my Father was and outlined our family tree. He paused and said he remembered my mother from Baidoa but could not recall ever meeting my Father.

'I welcome this news,' he said, gently. 'But I must speak with the rest of the family. Especially with her mother. Call me again next week.'

It was not a yes, it was not a no, but it was the beginning. I thanked him and ended the call.

Afterwards, I sat quietly by the window. I thought about our younger selves in Baidoa and then in Marka, meeting and chatting and laughing. I thought of the letters, the tears, the prayers. And now, decades later, I had just asked for her hand in marriage.

I called Hindiyeey.

'He was calm,' I told her. 'He listened. He said he would speak with your mother and the rest of the family. He asked me to call him next week.'

There was a pause at her end. Then I heard her crying softly.

'Alhamdulillah,' she whispered. 'Thank you, Sahal. I knew you would do it. I am very proud of you, my love.'

That night, I finally slept.

The Longest Week

The week that followed my call to Hindiyeey's Father was interminable. Each day crawled by with the weight of eternity, and I found myself checking my phone obsessively, even though I knew he would not call until the promised time. This waiting, this suspended animation between hope and fear, reminded me of only two other moments in my life: the excruciating months awaiting my asylum decision and the breathless weeks before learning whether I had received the scholarship to Germany. Somehow, this felt heavier: the others had been about my survival, my future, but this was about love, about the woman who had anchored my heart since we were teenagers walking through the streets of Baidoa and Marka.

I could not concentrate: work became mechanical, my conversations with Olu and Gunther superficial. Even my prayers felt fragmented, although I found myself turning to Allah more frequently, sometimes in the middle of mundane tasks, whispering 'Ya Allah, make this easy' under my breath.

Hindiyeey called every evening, and I could hear the tension in her voice too. 'How are you holding up?' she would ask, and I would lie and say I was fine, just as she lied when I asked her the same question. We were two people treading water in an ocean of uncertainty, trying to keep each other afloat with words neither of us fully believed.

Jabriil called on Sunday evening, exactly a week later, as he had promised, although I was supposed to be calling him. My hands trembled as I answered the phone.

'Sahal,' his voice came through, clear and measured. 'I have spoken with the family.'

My heart stopped.

'I am willing to give you my daughter's hand in marriage.'

The words hit me like sunlight breaking through storm clouds. I nearly dropped the phone.

'But,' he continued, and that single word brought me crashing back to earth, 'there are conditions. You must wait until you receive your legal papers in Germany, and Hindiyeey must secure hers as well. Only then can this marriage proceed properly.'

'Alhamdulillah,' I managed to say, my voice thick with emotion. 'Thank you, Aabo Jabriil. I accept your conditions completely.'

The conversation did not end there; three days later, Hindiyeey called, her voice tight with frustration.

'My mother disagrees with my Father's plan,' she said without preamble. 'She says if you want to marry me, you must come to Finland. She won't let her daughter move to another country, away from the family. She's adamant, Sahal. She says Germany is too far.'

My head spun. Finland? I had built my life in Germany, learned the language, found work and established routines. The idea of starting again in yet another country felt overwhelming.

'There's more,' Hindiyeey continued, her voice growing quieter. 'My uncle, the one who sponsored our family to come to Finland, has been pushing for me to marry his eldest son, Abdi. He just graduated from university here and has a good job. The family sees it as perfect: keeping everything within the family, ensuring I stay close to home.'

I felt the ground shifting beneath my feet. 'And what do you want?' I asked, though I was terrified of the answer.

'I want you,' she said fiercely. 'I've waited all these years for you, Sahal. I won't let them choose my husband for me, not even though they are my family. But the pressure is enormous.

Every day, someone is talking to me about Abdi, about how practical it would be, how much easier life would be.'

I consulted my parents that evening, my voice heavy with confusion. My Father listened patiently as I explained the situation.

'Finland might not be a bad idea,' he said thoughtfully. 'You would get papers more easily through marriage. But son,' his voice grew serious – my Father was a man of few words but always a straight talker, 'be careful not to lose yourself. When you marry into a family and move to where they live, you risk becoming absorbed into their sphere completely. You might find yourself more son-in-law than husband, more dependent than independent.'

My mother agreed. 'I like Hindiyeey's family, but a man needs to stand on his own feet. In our culture, when you move into the wife's family domain, the dynamics can become ... complicated.'

I talked to Olu and Gunther about it at our usual café. They meant well, but their advice felt superficial.

'Just follow your heart, man,' Olu said, clapping me on the shoulder.

'Yeah, love conquers all, right?' Gunther added with a grin.

But they did not understand the intricate web of family obligations, cultural expectations and community dynamics that governed our world. Their perspective, while well-meant, did not grasp the nuances of the Somali culture I was navigating.

Days turned into sleepless nights as I wrestled with the decision. Then, in a moment of clarity born of desperation, I thought of Martin, my lawyer. If I could reopen my asylum case and appeal against the previous rejection, perhaps I could secure my status in Germany and make my path forward easier.

Martin was sceptical but willing. 'Your case was weak before, but circumstances change. We can file an appeal based on the deteriorating conditions in Somalia and your deeper integration into German society. It's a long shot, but it's possible.'

Within a week, we had filed the appeal. With that decision made, everything else became clearer.

I called Jabriil. 'I've decided to stay in Germany and fight for my papers here. I want Hindiyeey to join me once I'm legal. I understand your condition about waiting for papers, and I respect it.'

There was a long pause. 'The family wants her in Finland,' he said finally.

'I understand, but this is what I believe is best for our future. I'm not asking you to go against your family, but I'm asking you to support what your daughter wants.'

Another pause, longer this time. 'My daughter has made her choice clear to me,' he said quietly. 'Against the wishes of her mother and uncle, I will honour her choice. You may marry Hindiyeey.' Hearing this was a dream come true.

I thanked Jabrill, 'Thank you, Aabe Jabriil,' I said numerous times before the call ended. After hanging up, I jumped up and down in my living room, stretching my hands towards the sky and thanking Allah repeatedly.

The *nikah* took place three weeks later in Helsinki. It was small, almost secretive – just immediate family and a handful of close friends. Hindiyeey's mother attended but barely spoke about me. Her uncle was conspicuously absent. The imam who performed the ceremony seemed to rush through the ritual, as if he too sensed the family tension.

I should have been there, standing beside my bride, but without legal papers, I could not travel to Finland. Instead, I named an elder in Helsinki as my *wakeel* (agent) to represent me, while I waited by my phone in Frankfurt, my heart aching as the minutes passed. Hindiyeey called me straight after the ceremony, her voice a mixture of joy and sadness.

'We did it, Sahal,' she whispered. 'I'm your wife now.'

'And I'm your husband, I love you,' I replied, although the words felt hollow in my empty apartment. We were finally married, bound not just by love but by a sacred commitment, yet I had missed the most important day of our lives.

The celebration was muted, the congratulations lukewarm from half the attendees. But over the phone, I could feel Hindiyeey's joy, her relief that we had finally made it official, despite all the obstacles. That evening, with my heart still racing from the reality of being married, I called my parents in Garissa. Despite missing my own nikah ceremony, I felt a joy I needed to share with the people who had raised me and supported me through everything.

'Aabo, Hooyo, Father, Mother,' I said when they both came to the phone, my voice bright with happiness. 'Alhamdulillah, I am calling to tell you that Hindiyeey and I are married. The ceremony took place today in Helsinki.'

The silence lasted barely a moment before my mother's voice erupted in celebration.

'Alhamdulillah! Alhamdulillah! My son is married!' I could hear the joy radiating down the phone connection. 'Oh, Sahal, we are so happy for you. Hindiyeey is a good girl from a good family. May Allah bless your marriage.'

My Father's voice was steady, warm with paternal pride. 'This is wonderful news, my son. You have chosen well, and she has chosen well. May Allah grant you both happiness and many years together.'

'We wish we could have been there,' my mother added, her voice thick with emotion. 'But Allah knows best. The important thing is that you are married now, officially husband and wife.'

'Make *dua* for us, Hooyo,' I asked, the weight of our separation already settling back onto my shoulders. 'Make *dua* that Allah makes it easy for us to be together soon.'

'Every day, my child,' she replied without hesitation. 'Every day I will make *dua* for you and Hindiyeey. May Allah bless your marriage, may He bring you together quickly, and may He grant you righteous children who will be the apples of your eye.'

My Father's voice joined in. 'And may Allah strengthen your bond, protect you both from harm, and make your marriage a source of peace and happiness for both families.'

Their prayers felt like a blessing washing over me, filling the emptiness of my Frankfurt apartment with warmth and hope. For those precious minutes on the phone, I was not a man separated from his new wife by impossible circumstances; I was simply a son sharing his joy with the parents who loved him.

After hanging up, I sat quietly for a long time, holding onto their happiness, their prayers, their unwavering support. Whatever challenges lay ahead, I knew my parents' *dua* would be with me every step of the way

Two days later, my new wife called me again, but she was still 1,500 kilometres away in Helsinki. We had won the battle to be together, but now faced the war of actually being apart. The irony was not lost on me; I had fought so hard to marry her, and yet I could not even attend my own *nikah* ceremony.

As I stared out of my window at the Frankfurt sky, I realised that getting married had been the easy part. The real test of our love was just beginning.

When Everything Falls Apart

Three months after our *nikah*, Martin's call came on a grey Tuesday morning in November, as I was getting ready for work. I knew as soon as he spoke, for his voice carried the weight of bad news.

'I'm sorry, Sahal. The appeal has been rejected.'

The words hit me in the stomach like someone physically punching me. I had pinned everything on this appeal, convinced myself that I would be lucky the second time around. Now the door had slammed shut, and I felt the walls of my small Frankfurt apartment closing in around me.

'What are my options now?' I asked, though my voice sounded distant, even to myself.

'Limited,' Martin admitted. 'We could try another appeal, but the chances are minimal. I'm sorry, truly.'

After hanging up, I called in sick to work. I could not face work, the responsibilities, the pretence of normality. I sat motionless for hours. This rejection felt like more than just a legal setback; it was a judgement on my worth, my future, my ability to provide for the woman I loved. The dream of bringing Hindiyeey to Germany, of building our life together in the country I had called home for the last two and a half years, had crumbled.

First, I called Hindiyeey. Her voice was bright when she answered, probably expecting our usual morning check-in.

'Sahal, Habibi, how are you?'

'The appeal was rejected,' I said without preamble. The words felt like stones in my mouth.

The silence stretched between us across the miles. When she finally spoke, her voice was gentle, consoling.

'Oh, my love, I'm so sorry. But this doesn't change anything between us. We'll find another way, inshallah.'

I could hear her trying to be strong for me, but something in her tone, a slight hesitation, a carefully controlled steadiness, made me wonder what she was not saying. Was she now having doubts? How could she not, with her family's constant pressure and now this definitive blow to our German dreams?

'What will we do now?' I asked.

'We'll work it out together,' she said, but the words felt rehearsed, like something she was telling herself as much as me.

Later that day, I knew I had to call Jabriil. This changed everything, given the conditions he had set, the promise I had made. My hands shook as I dialled his number.

'Aabo Jabriil,' I began, 'I need to tell you that my asylum appeal has been rejected.'

The silence was longer this time and heavier.

When he spoke, his voice carried a finality that made my blood run cold. 'Then there is only one option left, Sahal. You must come to Finland. I will not, and let me be absolutely clear about this, I will not send my daughter to a man in Germany who has no papers, no legal status, no future. If you want to be her husband in reality, not just on paper, you will have to come here.'

His words were delivered without anger, but with the unmistakable authority of a Father protecting his child. There was no room for negotiation, no softness in his tone.

'But Aabo...'

'No,' he cut me off. 'I have been patient. I allowed this marriage against the wishes of the rest of the family because I believed you would get your papers. That hope is now gone. Finland is your only option if you want to be with my daughter.'

The call ended with those words hanging in the air like a verdict.

That evening, I called my parents in Garissa, dreading their reaction but knowing they needed to hear it from me.

'My son,' my Father said after I explained everything, 'this is a test from Allah. Do not make hasty decisions in your despair.'

'But Aabo, what choice do I have? Jabriil says I must come to Finland or lose Hindiyeey forever.'

My mother's voice came through, firm and unwavering. 'Sahal, listen to me. Allah's timing is not our timing. What seems like a closed door may be Allah protecting you from something worse. Stay in Germany. Be patient. Something will come up.'

'But Hooyo, my marriage,' I said, in a desperate attempt to make sense of what was unfolding in my mind.

'Your marriage will survive if it is meant to be,' my Father interrupted. 'But don't throw away everything you've built in Germany out of panic. You have work there, you understand the system, and you speak the language now. Starting over in Finland ... that is not a small thing.'

Their conviction was absolute, but it felt like they were asking me to choose between their wisdom and my wife. After hanging up, I sat alone in my apartment, understanding that everyone I loved had drawn their lines in the sand, and I was caught in the middle with an impossible choice to make.

The impact on me was swift and brutal. At work, I found myself snapping at the car wash staff I supervised, my patience worn thin by the constant anxiety gnawing at me. Simple problems that I would normally solve with ease became mountains of frustration. When a customer complained about a delayed wash, I responded with barely concealed irritation instead of my usual diplomatic approach.

My line manager, Alket, who had always been supportive, pulled me aside after a particularly difficult week.

'Sahal, what's going on? This isn't like you,' he said, his voice concerned but cautious. 'Your performance has dropped significantly. The staff are complaining, and we've had three customer complaints this month alone.'

I wanted to explain everything – the rejected appeal, the separation from my wife, the impossible choices ahead – but the words stuck in my throat. How could I tell him that I was drowning?

'I'm going through some personal difficulties,' I managed to say.

Alket nodded slowly. 'Look, I want to help you get back on track. You're a good worker, and I don't want to lose you. But I need to see improvement. Can you do that?'

His words carried both support and warning. I could see the conflict in his eyes – he genuinely cared about me, but he also had a business to run. The irony was that he was worried I might leave, while I was trapped, unable to go anywhere.

The financial strain made everything worse. Every month, I sent what little extra I had to Hindiyeey – small gifts, money for her phone bill, anything to show that I was still her husband despite the distance. But my salary, which had once been enough to support both myself and my parents back in Garissa, was now stretched impossibly thin. I found myself counting German marks, skipping meals, and walking instead of taking the tram to save a few marks here and there.

Meanwhile, Hindiyeey's situation in Helsinki grew more difficult by the day. Her Father remained her steadfast ally, but the rest of the family were cold to her. Her mother barely spoke to her, and her siblings treated her like a stranger who had brought shame upon them by marrying me rather than her cousin.

'My uncle came to the house again yesterday,' she told me, during one of our increasingly strained phone calls. 'He was talking to my mother in the kitchen, but I could hear everything. He kept saying, "I told you this marriage was a mistake. Look at her now, married to a man who can't even visit her, who has no papers, no future."'

I could hear the exhaustion in her voice, the way doubt had begun to creep into her words.

'He's wrong,' I said, trying to inject a confidence I did not feel into my voice. 'This is temporary. We'll find a way.'

'When, Sahal? When will we find a way?' For the first time since I'd known her, Hindiyeey sounded defeated. 'My mother won't even eat meals with me anymore. Yesterday, she said maybe I should consider ...' She stopped herself.

'Consider what?'

'Nothing. It doesn't matter.'

But I knew what her mother had said. She should consider divorce, consider the uncle's son, consider that maybe everyone was right, and I was just a stubborn fool chasing an impossible dream.

My parents, calling from Garissa, remained firmly opposed to the idea of Finland, even though my appeal had been rejected.

'Son, don't make decisions out of desperation,' my Father counselled, during one of our weekly calls. 'Finland is not the answer. You'll become dependent on your wife's family and lose your independence. Find another way.'

'What other way, Aabo? Tell me what other way there is!'

My mother took the phone. 'Sahal, my child, I hear the anger in your voice. This is not like you. Trust in Allah's plan. Don't rush into decisions that will change your life forever.'

What they did not understand was that doing nothing was also a decision, a decision to watch my marriage crumble under the weight of separation and doubt.

Olu and Gunther noticed the change in me immediately. I had become withdrawn, declining their invitations to coffee, avoiding the casual conversations that had once been the highlight of our weekend. When they cornered me one afternoon, their concern was evident.

'Man, you're worrying us,' Olu said bluntly. 'You look like you haven't slept in weeks. When's the last time you ate a proper meal?'

'I'm fine,' I lied, but even I could hear how hollow the words sounded.

Gunther shook his head. 'No, you're not fine. Whatever's going on, you can talk to us. We're your friends.'

How could I explain the complexity of my situation to them? How could I make them understand the cultural expectations, the family pressures, the weight of being responsible not just for our happiness but for Hindiyeey's reputation, her future, her relationship with her family?

Instead, I retreated further into myself, finding solace in the only place that still felt reliable: my faith. Prayer became my anchor. I spread out my small prayer rug in my apartment and surrendered my worries to Allah. I found myself praying more often, whispering supplications while I was commuting to work, during my lunch break, before going to sleep, constantly making *dua* to Allah to grant me a way out of this impossible situation.

I called my parents more frequently now, not just for their advice but also to ask for their prayers.

'Hooyo, please make *dua* for me,' I would beg my mother. 'Ask Allah to make this easy.'

'Every day, my son,' she would reply. 'Every day I ask Allah to guide you to the right path.'

But as the weeks passed and no breakthrough came, I began to wonder whether perhaps the right path was the one I was most afraid to take. Maybe Finland was not a surrender; maybe it was the only way forward. Maybe love sometimes requires the sacrifice of everything you thought you wanted for the person who matters most.

The question that haunted my sleepless nights was not whether I loved Hindiyeey enough to move to Finland. It was whether I was strong enough to rebuild my life from scratch, again, in a third country, under the watchful eyes of a family that had never wanted me in the first place.

The Storm That Changed Everything

For three weeks, I lived in a state of suspended animation, caught between the immovable forces of family loyalty and marital duty. Each morning, I would wake with the weight of decision pressing down on my chest like a physical burden. Each night, I would lie awake staring at the ceiling, no closer to resolution than when the sun had risen.

My prayer rug became my refuge. Five times a day turned into six, then seven, then countless moments throughout each day when I would stop whatever I was doing and turn to Allah for guidance. I found myself whispering 'Rabbana ihdina – Our Lord, guide us' – while on my way to work, while supervising the car wash staff, while eating my solitary meals. Never in my life had I felt so desperately in need of divine intervention.

The choice seemed impossible because both paths led to betrayal. If I stayed in Germany, I would be failing as a husband, abandoning the woman I had fought so hard to marry. If I went to Finland, I would be disappointing my parents, who had sacrificed everything for my education and success, who had trusted me to make wise decisions even when the world seemed determined to crush my dreams.

Jabriil's words haunted me: 'I will not send my daughter to a man who has no future.' How could I argue with a Father's protective instinct? How could I ask him to trust his daughter's happiness to someone who could not even guarantee his own legal existence?

Yet my parents' counsel felt equally valid: 'Don't panic into throwing away everything you've built.' They were not wrong either. I had learned German, understood the system, built relationships, and found work. Starting over again in Finland would mean returning to square one – language barriers, cultural differences, and complete dependence on Hindiyeey's family, who had never wanted me in the first place.

As the days crawled by, I began to lean towards surrender – not because I was convinced it was right, but because the weight of disappointing Hindiyeey felt heavier than that of disappointing my parents. She was my wife now, my immediate responsibility. Perhaps love sometimes required the sacrifice of everything else you held dear. I was composing the words in my head, practising how I would tell my parents that I had decided to move to Finland, when everything changed.

It was a Thursday evening in late December when my phone rang. I did not recognise the number that appeared on the screen, but when I answered, it was Hindiyeey, I barely recognised her voice. It was raw, shaking with rage and exhaustion.

'Sahal, I can't do this anymore. I can't live in this house.'

'What happened? What's wrong?'

'My mother,' she said, her voice breaking. 'She's been at me all day, all week, telling me that I made a mistake, that I'm destroying the family, that I should consider Abdi before it's too late. And today, she said ...' She paused, taking a shuddering breath. 'She said maybe Allah is showing us through your rejected appeal that this marriage was never meant to be.'

My heart clenched. 'What did you say?'

'I lost it, Sahal. I screamed at her. I told her that I chose you, that I would choose you again, that no one–not her, not my uncle, not anyone—would make decisions about my life for me. And then I walked out.'

'Where are you now?'

'I'm at a friend's house. But I'm not going back, Sahal. I can't. I've already contacted social services. As an adult experiencing family conflict, I have the right to my own housing. They're going to help me get an apartment.'

I sat in stunned silence. My wife, my gentle, family-oriented wife who had always tried to please everyone, had just declared war on her own household.

'Are you sure about this?' I asked, although part of me felt a surge of relief. 'This is a big step, Hindiyeey. Once you do this, there's no going back.'

'I'm sure,' she said, and her voice was stronger now, more determined. 'I'm tired of being pulled in every direction by people who claim to love me but won't respect my choices. I'm tired of feeling guilty for choosing the man I love. I'm tired of living in a house where I'm treated like a child who made a foolish mistake.'

That night, I couldn't sleep. But for the first time in weeks, it wasn't because of the impossible choice hanging over me. It was because everything had suddenly shifted. Hindiyeey had taken control of her destiny and, in doing so, had freed me from the trap I'd been caught in.

Over the following days, she moved into a small studio apartment provided by social services. The break with her family was complete except for her Father, who, despite his disappointment, continued to speak to her. Her mother, her siblings, her uncle – they all treated her decision as a betrayal that could not be forgiven.

'How do you feel?' I asked her during one of our evening calls.

'Lonely,' she admitted, 'but also ... free. For the first time since we got married, I can think clearly without ten different voices telling me what I should do.'

Two weeks later, she called with news that changed everything again.

'I'm getting my papers,' she said, her voice bright with excitement. 'Finnish residency. It will be official in two months.'

We both saw the irony: while I remained trapped in legal limbo, my wife, who had been seen as the dependent one, the one who needed protection, was about to become the one with security, with options, with the legal right to build a life wherever she chose.

'What does this mean for us?' I asked.

'It means the choice is yours now,' she said simply. 'You can come to Finland, and we can build our life together here, in our own place, on our own terms. Or you can stay in Germany and keep fighting for your papers there. But Sahal, if you decide to stay, I need you to know that I'm not going to wait forever. I've learned that I can't live my life suspended between other people's expectations and my own happiness.'

As I hung up, I realised that the impossible choice I'd been agonising over for weeks had just been replaced by a different one. My wife was not the victim of circumstances any longer – she was a woman who had fought for her independence and won. Now she was offering me the chance to join her in that freedom, if I were only brave enough to take it.

The storm had passed, but in its wake, everything had changed. The question was no longer whether I could bear to disappoint my parents or her Father. The question was whether I was strong enough to choose love over fear, partnership over paralysis, and an unknown future over the all too familiar struggle.

The Point of No Return

For a week after Hindiyeey's call, I carried two futures in my mind like competing prayers. In one, I remained in Frankfurt, grinding through another appeal, another rejection, another year of legal limbo, while my wife built a new life without me. In the other, I abandoned everything I had struggled to build – the language that had taken me years to learn, the friendships that had sustained me, the small corner of Germany I had claimed as home – and started again in a country whose language I didn't speak, living near to the very family that did not want me. Neither choice felt like a victory; each was a form of surrender.

The answer came to me during Friday prayer at the small mosque near my apartment. As I listened to the *khutba*, clarity struck like lightning: Germany had rejected me twice. The asylum office, the appeals court, and the entire legal system had looked at my case and found me wanting. What was I holding onto? What future was I protecting by staying?

Hindiyeey, meanwhile, had her residency papers coming, her own apartment, her independence. She had already shown more courage in two weeks than I had managed in months of indecision. She was not asking me to choose between her and my objectives any longer; she was offering me the chance to choose love over stubbornness, partnership over pride. I could not hold on any longer; I had to make a decision, and the decision had been made. Early on the Sunday morning, I made the call that would change everything.

'Hindiyeey,' I said when she answered, not bothering with our usual pleasantries. 'I'm coming.'

The silence on the other end stretched for so long that I thought the connection had broken. Then I heard a sharp intake of breath, followed by something between a laugh and a sob.

'Are you serious? You're really coming?'

'Yes,' I said, and saying it out loud made it real, irreversible. 'Germany has made it clear that I have no future here. My future is with you, wherever that is.'

She cried then, openly and without embarrassment, and I found my own eyes brimming with tears that I had not allowed myself to shed during all those weeks of agonising.

'When?' she asked through her tears.

'As soon as I can arrange everything. A week, maybe two.'

'Oh, Sahal, I can't believe it. I've been so scared that...', she stopped herself.

'That what?'

'That you would choose Germany over me. That your parents' advice would win in the end.'

Her honesty cut me to the bone because it was partially true. If Germany had offered me even a sliver of hope, I might have stayed. But there comes a point when holding onto hope becomes another form of self-destruction.

Listen carefully,' she said, her voice turning serious. 'If you're stopped by the police during the journey, tell them that your wife lives in Helsinki and give them my address. I will get someone to compose a letter in Finnish explaining the situation. Keep it with you always.'

After hanging up, I sat in my apartment for an hour, looking around at the small space that had been my sanctuary for over two years. The prayer rug in the corner, the few photographs from home, the German language books I used to force myself to read until my eyes burned. All of it would soon be history.

The call to my parents was harder than I had expected.

'Aabo, Hooyo,' I began, then told them everything, about Hindiyeey's break from her family, her new apartment, her pending residency papers, and my decision to join her.

My Father's response surprised me. 'My son, you are facing an impossible situation with grace. We raised you to honour your commitments, and your wife is your first commitment now. If this is your only path forward, then walk it with your head high,' he said in his usual Bay Maay-Maay accent.

My mother's voice was gentler but equally supportive. 'Sahal, we worried that you were making this decision out of panic. But hearing you explain it now ... it sounds like a good plan, Hooyo. Trust in Allah's plan. He may be guiding you towards something better than what you're leaving behind.'

Their blessing lifted a weight that I had not even realised I was carrying.

Two days later, I called Gunther and Olu to my apartment. These men had become more than friends; they had been my guides to Germany and its culture, my companions during lonely months, my anchors to normality during the asylum process.

'I have to tell you something,' I said, before explaining everything.

Olu whistled softly. 'Man, that's a hell of a journey you're talking about. A train through Denmark and Sweden? That's going to take days.'

'I can't fly,' I explained. 'My asylum status'.

'We know,' Gunther interrupted. 'The question is, are you sure about this? Really sure?'

I nodded. 'Germany has made its position clear. Twice. I can't keep beating my head against a wall hoping that it will suddenly turn into a door.'

They exchanged glances, then Olu grinned. 'Well, if you're going to do something crazy, at least you're doing it for love. That counts for something.'

The next day, I walked into my manager's office and resigned. Alket looked genuinely sad to see me go.

'I wish things had worked out differently,' he said, shaking my hand. 'You're a good worker, Sahal. Whatever happens in your future, remember that.'

On my last evening in Frankfurt, I packed a single suitcase with essentials, locked my apartment, and handed the key to Olu.

'If I make it to Finland and settle there, consider everything in that apartment yours,' I told him. 'And if the housing association asks where I went, you don't know anything.'

He pocketed the key with a solemn nod. 'You'll make it, I will pray for you,' he said. 'And when you do, send us a postcard from Helsinki.'

The journey north began at dawn on a Tuesday, with a train ticket to Copenhagen clutched in my hand and Hindiyeey's letter folded carefully in my jacket pocket. I had no passport, no official documents that would allow me to travel, just the hope that the Schengen Agreement's open borders between Germany, Denmark, Sweden, and Finland would let me slip through unnoticed. As Frankfurt disappeared behind me, I felt the peculiar mixture of terror and liberation that comes with burning all your bridges at once – I was leaving Germany.

Three days of trains and buses lay ahead, trusting that border controls would remain invisible thanks to European unity. Three days would take me from one life into another, carrying nothing but hope and the promise of a woman who had already proven that she was braver than either of us had known.

As the German countryside rolled past my window, I whispered a prayer of gratitude for closed doors and impossible choices, for the blessings that sometimes come disguised as catastrophes, and for the woman waiting for me in Helsinki who had shown me that love, sometimes, requires the courage to lose everything in order to gain what matters most.

Part V – Arrival

Crossing into Hope

After three long and nerve-wracking days, I arrived in Helsinki safely. The journey had been a terrifying ordeal: every ticket inspection on the bus and train had brought the possibility of arrest. The most harrowing moment had come at the border between Sweden and Finland, when a uniformed officer stopped me. He looked at me hard, said something in Swedish, then nodded and let me pass without asking for papers. My legs trembled as I stepped away; it was a close call.

At Helsinki's main train station, I bought a phone card and found a quiet booth. My fingers were numb from the cold as I dialled Hindiyeey's number. When she answered, her voice was shaking.

'Sahal? Is it you? Are you safe?'

I could not speak at first. When I finally said 'Yes', she broke down. She told me that she had barely slept in days, fearing the worst. Her apartment was only ten minutes from the station, and she arrived breathless, a scarf around her neck, her eyes red with worry. We embraced tightly, kissed each other's cheeks, and, for a moment, the cold Helsinki wind faded away.

At her apartment, she made some tea and served me warm soup. Although I was exhausted from the journey, seeing her revived me. We talked for hours, catching up on the nearly four years we had lost. Her presence was comforting, yet the city felt alien and distant. I was safe with my wife, but the future was open-ended and not yet settled.

I called my parents in Garissa that evening. My mother answered. The moment she heard my voice, she began to pray aloud in gratitude. My Father came on the line next. His voice rattled with emotion. 'Alhamdulillah's. You made it, my son. May Allah protect you.'

A few days later, Hindiyeey took me to an immigration lawyer. He listened carefully, then shook his head. 'You can apply through family reunification, yes,' he said, 'but since Germany rejected you, Finland likely will too.' He was right. Three months later, I received my rejection letter. Memories of asylum rejections seemed to have followed me into Finland. 'What have I done to these countries? Why am I this unlucky? Why?' I whispered to myself after reading the letter.

The following morning, I called my parents to tell them about the rejection. My mother gasped, then whispered, 'Sahalow, Allah opens doors where we see only walls.' My Father was quieter, perhaps devastated, but said, 'You are not alone, my son. Take care of Hindiyeey. Don't give up.'

Despite the warmth at home, life in Helsinki without papers or work was unbearable. Hindiyeey and I were reunited, yes, but every day brought new hardship. I felt like a shadow in the city, invisible, undocumented, and increasingly desperate. To make matters worse, Hindiyeey's family, half of whom disapproved of our marriage, cut ties with both of us. I struggled with this deeply, but Hindiyeey remained composed. Her strength surprised me. She said, 'They may leave us, but we won't leave each other.'

I tried to reach out to her family, especially to her Father, Jabriil. I met him once briefly, but it was an awkward encounter. He was polite but distant, his eyes avoiding mine. He offered no warmth, no blessing. I had hoped for a softening, but none came. After that meeting, I gave up trying.

Six months after arriving, I received unexpected news: I was allowed to work. I found a job stacking shelves in a supermarket. It was quiet, lonely work. I rarely spoke to anyone, moving between the stockroom and the aisles like a ghost, but at least I earned something, which gave me a little dignity, a little hope.

Then, a year after I arrived, Hindiyeey became pregnant. The news was both joyous and frightening. She was often unwell, and our finances were stretched thin. We were still isolated from her family, and I was the only person to look after her. I felt like I was failing her, failing our unborn child, and failing my parents, who still depended on me in Garissa.

It was around that time that I met Yusuf, a Somali man who often helped new arrivals with housing and translation. We met at the mosque one evening. He was older and wore a thick leather jacket that smelled of cloves and oud. He listened to my story without interrupting, then leaned towards me.

'Your best hope is the UK,' he said bluntly. 'They ask fewer questions. Community is strong. You can work. You can live. People make it there.'

I hesitated. I had heard such promises before but had never believed them. Perhaps though I was wrong about the UK; maybe this is where Hindiyeey, I, and our unborn child were destined to be.

'I can help you and your wife. A real chance. Passport, ticket, all under your names. Trust me.' Everything he said was too good to be true, but he came across as convincing and trustworthy.

That night, I told Hindiyeey everything. She was lying on the bed, one hand on her belly. I sat beside her, unsure how to even begin. She listened quietly, then turned to me.

'Sahal,' she said softly, 'we didn't come this far to stop now. If there's a door, even a small one, we walk through it. Together. Ask about the money, how much it will cost us?' she said.

We said an *Istikhara* prayer that night. In the morning, we both had peace in our hearts.

I called my parents the next day. This time, I told them about our plan to leave Finland for the UK.

'You're doing what you must,' my Father said. 'Keep her safe. Keep the child safe.'

Then something unexpected happened, we received a phone call from Hindiyeey's family. Her younger brother was on the line. He spoke carefully, gently. 'Abaayo, we want to see you. All of you.'

We were invited to meet the whole family. I was hesitant, but Hindiyeey insisted we go. We arrived nervously, not knowing what to expect, but the atmosphere was warm. Her mother embraced her first, crying openly. Her Father stood behind, watching us. When I approached him, he did not look away but, this time, held my hand firmly. He did not say much, but the look in his eyes had changed.

That evening, we sat together as a family. We talked, shared food and, for the first time, laughed. The silence of the past year melted away. By the end of the visit, they had given us their blessing. Our marriage was acknowledged, and our decision to move to the UK was not only respected but also supported materially.

After we left Hindiyeey's family that evening, her Father called us. His voice, usually measured and formal, was full of warmth and resolve. 'We've talked as a family,' he said. 'We will support you. Don't worry about the cost; we'll pay the man who's arranging your trip to the UK.' His words lifted a weight I had not fully realised I was carrying.

The next day, I met Yusuf, who had been waiting patiently for my decision. I told him we were ready. He explained the process and asked me to bring him two passport-size photos of me and Hindiyeey. The process moved quickly. A week later, he handed us two Finnish passports with our names and photos and two round-trip tickets to London Heathrow. I held them in my hands; they were thin, official and unbelievably real. For the first time in years, an exit from this limbo felt possible.

The next morning, the sky was grey and heavy. We packed what little we had. At the airport, we moved with nervous calm, rehearsing our roles over and over again, but there were no issues, no questions. The plane lifted into the sky without any problems for us.

We landed in London quietly; there was no trouble at the border, no interrogations. The air was damp and thick with life. We did not linger, but that same day, we took a bus to Manchester. As the bus rumbled northwards, Hindiyeey leant her head on my shoulder. Her eyes were closed; her hand rested lightly on her belly. For the first time in a long while, I allowed myself a breath of hope.

Starting Over in Manchester

Manchester welcomed us not with bright lights and riches, but with a kind of quiet familiarity that grew on us day by day. After spending three nights in a small bed and breakfast that we had booked, we were tired, disoriented, and unsure of what lay ahead. But on the fourth day, as if Allah had placed him on our path, we met a Somali immigration lawyer at the community centre. His name was Kaahin, and he had been in the UK for nearly three decades. He spoke calmly, listened patiently, and assured us that he would help us complete fresh asylum applications now that we had arrived in the UK through irregular means.

'You are not the first, and you won't be the last,' he told us, smiling gently at Hindiyeey, who was clearly exhausted and struggling with her pregnancy.

Within a week, Kaahin had helped us submit our asylum claims, and we were advised to apply for accommodation and living support. Just three days later, we were moved into a council flat in the heart of Manchester. The block looked tired and worn down, with a broken fence and litter at the entrance, but it was our home now. The flat itself was in poor condition: the wallpaper was peeling, the carpet smelled damp, and the kitchen sink leaked constantly. When the housing officer saw that Hindiyeey was pregnant, he arranged for repairs to be carried out. Within a few weeks, we had new floors, fresh paint on the walls, and even a small cot delivered by a local charity shop.

The Somali community in Manchester was strong and visible. On the high street, we saw halal butchers, Somali cafés and money transfer shops tucked between old pubs and betting shops. I connected with the community elders at the mosque, exchanged stories with young men at the café, and slowly started to understand the rhythm of this new life. We had to rely nevertheless on our own initiative: no one was handed success; everyone had a story of hardship, of long nights and hard work.

While Hindiyeey mostly stayed at home, since her health remained fragile, and the pregnancy was not easy, I wandered the streets of Manchester, not in despair, but in quiet exploration. I looked for places to study, places to work, places where I could build something again. I walked along the River Irwell, past the university buildings, the libraries, and the job centres. Every corner of the city held possibilities.

At night, I called my parents in Garissa. I told them how different the UK felt – colder, faster, more structured, but also full of potential. 'Aabo,' I told my Father, 'This country moves quickly, but if you keep pace, you can build something real here.'

Despite the distance, I felt a closeness to home that I had not known in years. With Hindiyeey beside me, with her quiet strength and calm belief that everything would resolve itself, I felt that this country had been our destination all along. In all those years of moving between European cities, rejections, and waiting for a miracle, Manchester had been calling.

As new asylum applicants, we were allowed to attend college to study English. The college was near the city centre, and I received a bursary to cover my travel costs. My class was a mix of Africans – mostly Somalis, Eritreans, and Sudanese – and a few Middle Eastern students. I quickly realised that I spoke better English than most of my classmates, but I did not let that make me complacent. I wanted more than a level that would enable me to survive; I wanted to speak, write, and understand the language at a level that would open doors.

Six months passed. The days were long but filled with purpose. Then, one cold morning, we received a letter from the Home Office. Our asylum applications had been accepted: we were granted refugee status.

The joy we felt is impossible to describe. We sat in silence at first, reading the letter again and again. Then we laughed. Then we cried. We called our families in Garissa and Helsinki. My Father became very emotional, repeating 'Alhamdulillah, Alhamdulillah' over and over again. Now we had a future. We could begin to plan, not just survive. We could work legally, study without fear, and build a life for our child.

Just one week later, on a rainy Tuesday morning, Hindiyeey went into labour. I held her hand through every hour at the hospital, whispering prayers, wiping her forehead. Then, as the afternoon sun broke through the clouds, we heard the cry of our son – a strong, healthy boy. We named him Samatar.

Holding him in my arms, I felt something I had not felt in years – peace. The journey had been long, and we were still only at the beginning of a new chapter, but in that small council flat in Manchester, our newborn son asleep between us, we knew we were exactly where we were meant to be.

The Birth of Samatar

The birth of our son, Samatar, was the defining moment of our new life in Manchester: after all the turmoil, all the running, and all the uncertainty, holding that little boy in my arms made it all suddenly feel worthwhile. Hindiyeey had gone into labour a week after our asylum was granted, and the NHS staff had taken good care of her. When I first saw Samatar, my heart melted. He was a quiet baby with curious eyes and soft features, which reminded me so much of his mother. We named him Samatar- *He who helps with goodness*-a name rooted in hope and strength.

As soon as he was born, I picked up the phone and called my family in Garissa. My Father answered. The moment I told him that he had become a grandfather, there was silence on the line; then came the sound of his tears. It was a powerful moment – the circle of life had turned once more. I had fulfilled the promise I made to him years ago, in a way I could never have imagined. I called Hindiyeey's family in Helsinki, too, and they were overwhelmed with joy. Their daughter had become a mother, and in a new land that had once been a dream but was now our home.

Two days later, Hindiyeey and Samatar were discharged from the hospital; both were healthy and radiant. I brought them home to our small but freshly renovated council flat. Over the next two weeks, I became a full-time carer – changing nappies, heating bottles, and learning how to soothe a crying baby at 3 am. We barely slept. Samatar had his days and nights confused: he would nap through the day but stay alert and active through the night. Still, there was joy – a calm, overwhelming joy that seemed to hug our little home.

Four weeks after Samatar's birth, we received a visit that meant the world to us: Jabriil, Hindiyeey's Father, flew in from Helsinki. Pride and reassurance radiated from him, filling our modest flat. Watching him hold Samatar for the first time, tears welling in his eyes, was a proud moment for Hindiyeey. For that one week he stayed with us, the flat was filled with laughter, stories, and the wisdom of a grandfather meeting his first grandchild. When he returned to Helsinki, we felt both gratitude and loneliness – but the seed of family was now planted in our Manchester soil.

As our life started to settle into a routine, I knew that I had to keep building. Hindiyeey was still recovering and mostly stayed at home with Samatar. I rearranged my schedule, switching my English lessons to the evenings so I could look for work during the day. That is how I landed my first job in the UK, in a warehouse, loading and unloading lorries. It was backbreaking work, the toughest I had done in my life, but it paid the bills. I stuck with it for six months, determined to provide for my family. Every evening, I would head to my English class, exhausted but focused. I was the best English speaker in my class, especially among the Somali and African students, but I was determined to polish my skills further. I knew English would be the key to unlocking something bigger.

And then, one small opportunity changed everything. I applied for a temporary data analyst position with a local refugee charity. They liked my English and my organisational skills, and I got the job. It was my first desk job and my first taste of working with computer systems. That job lit a fire in me: I became fascinated with databases, spreadsheets and software tools. I would stay behind after work, just exploring the programmes on the office computer.

That curiosity led me to enrol in a Diploma in Programming the following academic year. It was a course funded by the

European Union, designed to prepare adult learners like me for work in tech or further education. I soaked up every lesson, every line of code. I finally felt that I had found my direction, my calling.

Upon completing the diploma, I was promoted to a job as Database Administrator at the same charity. The work was more technical now, and being methodical, problem-solving, and forward-thinking, I was good at it. I was beginning to see my future clearly and loved what I was doing.

At home, Hindiyeey and Samatar thrived in their own way. Our flat had become a safe, happy space. Samatar was growing quickly, curious about everything. His first word was 'abaayo' – a word he heard Hindiyeey repeat often on phone calls to her sister. We went for short walks in the local park or, sometimes, just sat by the window and watched the world go by.

When I completed my diploma, I applied to and was accepted onto a part-time BSc course in computing at the University of Manchester. I remember standing at the gates of the university, feeling disbelief that I had gone from being a refugee to a student again. It was a four-year programme, but I was ready for the long road ahead. Those four years were some of the most demanding of my life. I juggled fatherhood, work, studies, and the emotional burden of supporting my ageing parents in Garissa. My salary barely stretched. Some days, I would skip meals so we could afford nappies or a phone card for international calls to my parents, but I never once considered quitting. The vision was clear now: I was building something for all of us.

Through it all, Samatar continued to grow and became the centre of our world. Every small milestone – his first steps, his first laugh, his first haircut – felt like a reward for all the sacrifices we had made. I would sometimes sit on the floor with him, my textbooks open beside his toy cars, and imagine the life he would one day have – a life better than ours, one of choices, dignity and peace.

We were no longer just survivors. We were a family – building, learning and thriving in a city that had once felt cold but was slowly becoming our home.

First Class Degree

The day I graduated was not a loud and colourful moment, but it was deeply meaningful and quietly powerful in a way I had never imagined. It had taken me four long years of part-time study, evening lectures, late nights typing up assignments after Samatar had fallen asleep, and long days of juggling work, family, and study. But here I was, on a rainy morning in Manchester, wearing a black gown and cap, standing among other graduates in the university hall.

As I stood in the line waiting to be called up, I thought about the journey that had brought me here – not just from Dadaab or Helsinki, but all the way from that dusty schoolyard in Baidoa where Macalin Adan Dheere had once told me, 'You have a mind that must travel further than your feet ever will.' I had carried that sentence through years of movement, loss, love, war and healing, and now my mind had indeed travelled far – across languages, systems and pain to earn this piece of paper they called a degree.

The ceremony itself was short, formal, and somewhat impersonal, but when they called my name and I walked up to shake the Vice Chancellor's hand, I felt something rise within me–not pride, exactly, and not happiness, but something quieter and deeper, a silent affirmation that my life had not been in vain.

Hindiyeey was sitting in the second row of the hall, her hijab wrapped neatly, a wide smile on her face. She held Samatar on her lap. He was now almost five, his little legs dangling, his eyes darting around the hall. When he saw me go up on the stage, he clapped, although no one else was clapping. I caught his eye, smiled, and waved gently. That moment alone was the reward: no applause, no speech, and no spotlight, just my son looking at me as if I had done something worth remembering.

After the ceremony, we went home. There was no big party, just a quiet meal, a simple cake from a Somali shop, and a few friends who came by to say congratulations. One of them, an old man named Abshir who worked as a taxi driver, pulled me aside and said,

'You've become something good, my son. We must never forget where we started.'

Later that evening, after the guests had left and Samatar had fallen asleep on the sofa, I went into the small spare room we used as a study. I sat at the desk, opened my old notebook – the one I had carried around since my English classes – and wrote a short letter that I would never send.

'Aabe,
I did it.
I know you may never fully understand what a degree in computing means, but I know you would be proud. I still remember the promise I made to you in Marka that I would not waste my life, that I would carry our family's honour forward. Today I kept that promise.

There were times I wanted to give up – when my back hurt from lifting boxes in the warehouse, when I missed deadlines because Samatar was ill, or when Hindiyeey was exhausted and we had only £40 to stretch for the whole week – but we held on.

Tell Mum that I remembered her *dua*. Tell her that I remembered her every time I was tired and hungry and alone in a computer lab.

I will teach Samatar everything you taught me – to stand up, to work hard, and to keep faith.

I came out of the darkness. I walked a long road. I reached the light–not the one at the end of the tunnel, but one at the end of a chapter. I closed the notebook, kissed its cover and sat back in my chair. The house was quiet, warm and peaceful. Outside, Manchester rain fell on the window; inside, I knew deep in my heart that the worst of the struggle was behind us.

This was not the end of the story, but it was the end of a long chapter. The boy who had been forced to leave Baidoa had now become a man, a graduate, a Father, and a husband in Manchester. And perhaps, just perhaps, this country – so far from home – was no longer a place where we were simply surviving; it was becoming the place we belonged.

Sahal Software

After I graduated with my degree in computing, I found work as a web developer in a local media company in Manchester. It felt like a dream – doing what I loved, writing lines of code, solving real-world problems, and earning a decent wage. For the first time since our arrival in the UK, we felt financially secure. I would come home from work to find Samatar waiting by the window, ready to tell me all about his day. Hindiyeey had regained her energy, and our small flat buzzed with warmth and purpose.

Two years passed quickly. Samatar started school, a milestone that touched me more than I had expected. I remember holding his tiny hand as we walked to the school gate that first morning, his backpack nearly half his size, his eyes wide with curiosity. He turned to me and said, 'Baba, I'm going to be smart like you.' That sentence stayed with me for days.

One evening, after we had put Samatar to bed, Hindiyeey and I sat down in the living room, sipping tea. The room was quiet except for the occasional sound of a passing car. I looked at her and said, 'My love, Samatar is starting school. I love my job and, as you know, it pays well, and we are doing okay, but I have an idea that's been simmering away for the last couple of months.'

She looked at me and raised an eyebrow, smiling. 'Two months and you didn't tell me?'

I chuckled. 'I wasn't ready yet. But hear me out.'

'Okay,' she said, putting down her cup and giving me her full attention.

'I've been thinking about quitting my job and starting my own software company. I've got a few colleagues who might come in as small investors. It's risky, and we could lose everything ... but on the other side of the coin, it could work. We could build something meaningful – something that's ours.'

She was silent for a moment, then said, 'I was thinking of studying again too – improving my English, maybe enrolling in a teaching degree at the Open University ... but now you're planning to quit your job?'

I nodded slowly, not sure what she would say.

She looked at me, her face softening. 'I'll delay my studies for a year and see how it goes. I'm happy to support you.' In that moment, I realised again how central she was to my life, with her quiet strength, her trust in me, and her patience. Without Hindiyeey, I would have been a different man, walking a much lonelier path.

Within six months, I had secured sufficient investment to get started. I left my job and registered my business, Sahal Software, with Companies House. The company started small, offering basic IT training for job seekers. Most of our clients were adult learners referred by local job centres, and their tuition fees were covered by government schemes.

The early months were tough: I worked late into the night, preparing lesson plans, fixing broken printers, dealing with invoices, and the endless paperwork. We started with just two classrooms and three instructors, but word spread quickly in the community. Our students felt welcome and respected. Many were like me – starting over, uncertain but determined.

Within a year, we had grown so much that we employed ten teachers and three course administrators. We offered training in web development, office applications, and computer literacy. We were even awarded a small contract to deliver apprenticeships for young people in Greater Manchester.

Meanwhile, Samatar was flourishing in school. His teachers praised his curiosity and creativity. He was especially good at mathematics and had developed a love for storytelling, often writing short, funny poems that he would read to us over dinner. I saw myself in him, but also something brighter – a future I once dared not imagine.

That same year, Hindiyeey completed her English course and finally began her part-time teaching degree through the Open University. Every evening, she would sit at the kitchen table with her books open, writing essays and lesson plans, while Samatar played quietly nearby. I was proud of her beyond words. Watching her commit to learning again, after everything we had been through, filled me with admiration.

Five years later, she completed her degree. I remember the day she received her certificate by post. She opened the envelope slowly, as if unsure whether it was real. Then, with tears in her eyes, she held it up and said, 'I did it.' We hugged for a long time in the living room, not saying anything, just holding each other.

Soon afterwards, she was offered a teaching job at a local primary school: a perfect fit. She loved working with children, especially those who were new to England or struggling to adjust. Her own experience made her a compassionate and patient teacher. For the first time since we arrived in the UK, we were both doing work that fulfilled us.

Samatar had just completed Year 6 and was getting ready to start secondary school. He was excited, nervous, and ready for the challenge. On his last day at primary school, he brought home a small trophy for 'Best Effort in English'. I took a photo of him holding it, his smile wide and bright. That evening, he said, 'Baba, one day I want to work in your company.'

I laughed and said, 'We'll see, my boy. Maybe one day you'll run it.'

As Sahal Software continued to grow, expanding into new areas and training more students, I often found myself thinking back to the night I shared my dream with Hindiyeey in the living room. That simple conversation had changed everything. We were not simply surviving any longer; we were building, not only for ourselves, but for our son, for our families back home, and for a community that had once opened its arms to us when we had nothing but a glimmer of hope.

A House in the Trees

Sahal Software continued to thrive. Contracts were flowing in steadily, and the number of students enrolled in our training programmes had doubled within two years. From a humble rented office with plastic chairs and second-hand computers, we had grown into a recognised name in community-based digital education. It was something to be proud of. Even as the company grew, though, even as money came in more steadily and our work was praised by local agencies and educational institutions, both Hindiyeey and I felt a mild disquiet. It was not burnout, nor was it boredom. It was a longing for something more enduring than the next contract, something more meaningful than profit margins and company growth charts. We felt it especially strongly in the evenings when Samatar came home from school, his backpack slung over his shoulder, asking questions about space, coding, or the lives of people in other countries. He had an insatiable curiosity, one that reminded me of the boy I once was, sitting on the dusty floor of Baidoa, dreaming of a world far beyond the town's cracked roads.

Samatar was due to start secondary school. He had done well in his SATs, and his teachers described him as diligent, inquisitive, and imaginative – a child with great potential. One evening, as we sat in the kitchen, sipping tea and watching the sun retreat behind the rooftops, I turned to Hindiyeey and said, 'My love, it's time for something new.'

She looked up from her cup, the same gentle look that had comforted me through every storm. 'What are you thinking?' she asked.

'I think we've done well with Sahal Software,' I said. 'We built something beautiful. But I want us to do something more meaningful now, something lasting. Samatar is growing, and we have the means to give him the kind of opportunities we never had. And beyond that, I want us to help others do the same.'

We talked late into the night, like we did in the early days, before life pulled us in so many directions. It was a heartfelt discussion, deep and emotional. We both knew we were standing at a new threshold. By the end of the conversation, our minds were made up.

Within two months, we began the process of selling our shares in Sahal Software. It was not an easy decision. I had built that company with my bare hands and sleepless nights. It was the first thing I had ever owned that truly felt like mine, but letting go was not a loss; rather, it was a kind of giving.

We used the proceeds to buy a house in a quiet, leafy part of South Manchester, the kind of neighbourhood where children rode bikes on the pavement, and neighbours smiled at each other from behind tall hedges. The house had a garden with two old apple trees and enough space for Samatar to have his own room with a desk by the window. When we moved in, he ran from room to room with joy, opening and closing the doors as if he were claiming his castle.

We also enrolled him in a fee-paying private school. It was a carefully chosen institution that valued curiosity as much as results, where the classes had no more than twenty pupils, and teachers were known to stay after hours to help students prepare for the future. We did not make this decision lightly. We knew what it meant. It was not about prestige, but about placing him in an environment where his potential would be stretched and nurtured, where he would carry the torch of our family story into a future we could only imagine.

At the same time, we launched a non-profit organisation, Himilo Mentorship Network. 'Himilo' means ambition, and that is what we hoped to inspire. Our mission was clear: to support Somali youth in Greater Manchester to find direction, confidence, and success in education, employment, and integration. We offered mentorship programmes, career guidance, workshops on university applications, CV clinics, and summer internships. We matched young people with Somali professionals – doctors, teachers, IT specialists, and business owners – people who had once stood where these young Somalis stood, uncertain, overlooked, full of dreams but unsure where to begin.

The response was overwhelming. Within months, we had over one hundred active mentees. Some were teenagers still in school, others were young adults struggling to find meaningful work or applying for university. They came with questions, but also with stories, stories of migration, lost fathers, language barriers, and resilience.

Our small office in Moss Side became a hive of activity. On any given afternoon, young men and women would be engaged in mock interviews, and older mentors would discuss career goals over tea, and sometimes offer simple, silent companionship, helping a young person to feel, perhaps for the first time, that they belonged.

For me, it was a deeply personal project. Each young man who walked through that door reminded me of my younger self – the young man who had stood, confused, in a refugee camp with just a paper bag of belongings. I mentored dozens of them personally. I told them my story, not to impress them but to show them that where you begin does not define where you end.

Hindiyeey became the heart and soul of the organisation: she left her previous job, took up a part-time teaching role at a local primary school, and devoted the rest of her time to Himilo. Her warmth and openness were magnetic. The young women gravitated towards her, not just as a mentor but as a role model, a mother, a teacher, someone who believed in their worth.

Samatar, now twelve, had begun to grow into a confident, thoughtful boy. He loved his new school, especially the science labs and the music room where he was learning to play. As we walked to school one crisp autumn morning, he said, 'Aabo, I want to be a scientist. Or maybe an inventor.' I smiled and said, 'Be both.'

Our lives had changed – from the cramped flat in Longsight where we had struggled to afford heating, to this leafy street where our son played football with Oliver, Yusuf, and Charles, his neighbours. What truly mattered, though, was not the postcode or the size of the garden – it was the purpose we had found in giving back.

Our evenings were no longer about business meetings and deadlines; they were about community, about Himilo, about the children who still needed someone to believe in them. We were no longer chasing success; we were building a legacy.

Part VI – Legacy

Part VI - Lesson

The Day My Father Died

About five in the morning, one Sunday, the phone rang. Although the house was still wrapped in the silence of sleep, Hindiyeey was already awake in the kitchen, sipping water; she'd been battling a cold that week and often woke up early. I was still in bed, caught between dreams and the pull of dawn. Samatar lay sound asleep in his room, curled up under his duvet. He had a football match later that afternoon, but there was no urgency in the house yet; hours of relaxation stretched ahead.

The phone rang three times, then stopped. Then it rang again, twice.

Hindiyeey picked it up. At that hour, it could only be a call from Africa. No one local or even from Europe would be calling us at that time. My parents rarely rang early, which in itself made this call unsettling. I stirred in bed, listening.

A male voice came down the line, sharp and urgent. He asked for me by name.

'I'm his wife,' Hindiyeey replied hesitantly. 'Can I take a message?'

'It's urgent,' the man said. 'Something serious has happened. We need to speak to him.'

By then, I was wide awake, already out of bed, my heart racing, with a feeling of dread in my stomach. There was no logic to my fear, but it settled in me with cold certainty. I entered the kitchen in time for Hindiyeey to pass the phone to me, her face drained of colour.

The voice on the line was steady, sombre.

'Sahal,' it said, 'your Father passed away a few hours ago. I'm sorry for your loss. May Allah have mercy on his soul.'

For a moment, I could not believe it; I heard the words, but my mind rejected them. I stood still, as if caught in a nightmare from which I might soon wake. But I did not wake; this was real.

Hindiyeey gasped and broke down in tears, her hands covering her face. I held the phone tighter, willing the voice to speak again, to explain.

'What happened?' I asked.

'He was rushed to hospital,' the man said gently, 'but he passed away suddenly. We don't know the cause yet. Your mother... she's grief-stricken. She can't speak right now. But we'll call you again soon.'

'I'll call back shortly,' I replied. My voice was dry, as though the shock had drained all moisture from my body.

I sat beside Hindiyeey and wrapped my arm around her shoulders, trying to steady us both. She was sobbing loudly now, shattering the stillness of the morning. I rose, went to the bathroom, made *wudu*, and prayed two *rakah*. I asked Allah to have mercy on my Father, to ease his journey into the hereafter, and to give us the strength to be patient. My tears flowed freely, warm against my cheeks, but I felt unusually calm, as if my soul had temporarily surrendered to Allah's decree.

The noise must have woken Samatar. He emerged from his room, still in his pyjamas, rubbing his eyes.

'What's wrong, Mum?' he asked.

Hindiyeey could only pull him close and cry into his small shoulder.

I knelt beside them and told him as gently as I could, 'Your grandfather in Garissa passed away, Samatar.'

His face twisted in confusion and sadness. Then the tears came. He had never met his grandfather, but had heard his name many times from me. Samatar was old enough to grasp the weight of death, but still young enough for it to feel impossibly heavy.

By the afternoon, I managed to speak with my mother. Her voice was faint and distant, like wind moving through dry leaves. She spoke slowly, with long pauses. 'He went back to his Lord, Sahal,' she said. 'We cannot question His will. Make *dua* for him.'

Her strength in her grief moved me more than anything. She had lost the love of her life, the man she had shared everything with, yet her words were those of someone who had seen enough of life to understand that death, though painful, was part of the design.

That same evening, we began planning our trip. We could not arrive in time for the funeral – that was already over. In our traditions, burial follows swiftly after death, but we could still go. We *had* to go. We would visit his grave. We would sit with my mother. We would mourn together.

We took Samatar out of school for two weeks. It was not even a decision; it was instinct. He belonged with us. This was not just my loss or Hindiyeey's loss; it was our family's loss. We flew out two days later. The journey was long, heavy with the weight of grief. Airports blurred into each other, and even the sun felt dimmer in the places we passed through. When we finally reached Garissa, it was as though time had paused.

My mother waited for us in the front room, where my Father had spent much of his afternoons. Her back was straighter than I expected, her eyes swollen but dry. She held me tightly, her hands trembling. We sat side by side without speaking for a long time. Samatar leant against her knee, and she ran her fingers through his hair.

'My son,' she whispered eventually, 'he was so proud of you. He followed your every step, even when he didn't say it.'

I nodded, unable to reply.

That afternoon, we visited my Father's grave. The earth was still fresh. I knelt beside it, placing my hands against the soil, and whispered prayers into the warm dust, feeling both his presence and his absence. Samatar stood beside me, holding a bottle of water we had bought at the market to spray on the grave. He poured the water gently at the head of the grave.

Later that evening, my mother told stories about my Father: how he once gave his last money to a stranger on the road; how he loved to sing old Maay-Maay songs while shaving; how, even in old age, he never missed *Fajr* prayers. Hindiyeey listened closely, her hand in mine. Samatar asked questions, wanting to know more about the man he had never met.

In those two weeks, our mourning became a kind of healing. We cried; we prayed; we remembered. We served tea to guests who came to pay their condolences. We recited the Quran at dusk. We sat under the shade of the trees in the courtyard, letting the wind speak where our words failed.

When it was time to return to England, I kissed my mother's forehead and promised to call her every day. 'We are here for you, mum,' I said.

'I know,' she whispered. 'Your Father would have been proud of you, Sahal. Now carry his name with dignity, be charitable and kind.'

And so, we returned, changed. Grief had added a new note to our lives – deep, soft, constant, and charitable. My Father was gone, but his presence would echo in every prayer, every lesson I passed to Samatar, and every time I reached out to my mother's fading voice across the ocean.

May Allah have mercy on his soul. Amen.

The Light We Leave Behind

We returned to the UK on a grey Thursday morning. The sky over Heathrow was overcast, and the air felt heavier than usual, as if the grief we carried had followed us across continents. Hindiyeey rested her head against the window of the taxi as we drove to Manchester from the airport. Samatar sat between us, unusually quiet, his eyes fixed on the blur of motorway lights. None of us spoke much, but our silence spoke volumes.

The days that followed were slow, quiet and thick with reflection. The world went on, people sent their condolences and then slipped back into their routines, but something had shifted for me. Losing my Father – may Allah have mercy on him – had torn the fabric of my world. I was in my early fifties, healthy by Allah's mercy, but I found myself thinking more about time, what we leave behind and how little control we have over the moment for our passing.

In the early mornings, long before Samatar or Hindiyeey woke up, I would sit on the prayer mat in the living room, the Quran open in front of me. Sometimes I would read aloud, sometimes sit in stillness, making *istighfar*, seeking forgiveness from the Most Merciful. Some days I wept silently, not just for my Father but for all that I had left unsaid, the embraces I had postponed, the visits I had delayed. I thought of my mother back in Garissa, now sleeping alone in the house where my Father had once led prayers. Her voice over the phone was steady, but I knew she carried her grief in ways she did not share.

Samatar had returned to school a few days after our return, although he had been unwilling. I understood: he was still processing the visit to Garissa, the graveyard where we stood in silence, the image of his grandmother, wrapped in patience, standing next to me. For Samatar, that trip was about more than mourning – it was his first encounter with unfamiliar roots. He had never met his grandparents or been to Garissa or Baidoa. Those places were part of his story, but foreign to him. And yet, as we walked the red dust paths of Garissa, greeted by my parents' neighbours, I saw something settle in him.

Back at school, trouble found him – or perhaps he found it. A teacher accused him of being rude, of skipping detention, of having a 'bad attitude'. When the school emailed me, I did not believe it at first. Samatar, for all his restlessness, was a thoughtful boy. Yes, he had his moments, but he was never disrespectful. Hindiyeey was furious when she heard, but I told her to wait and let me handle it.

I took the morning off work and went to the school the next day. I met with the Head of Year and the teacher involved. I sat there, calm but firm. I told them plainly that I knew my son. I told them about what we had just been through, the trip we had made, the man we had buried. I reminded them that children carry grief differently, some in silence, some with sharpness, but I also reminded them that he was still a child, and that he was trying.

To their credit, they listened. Apologies were made. A new pastoral support teacher was assigned to keep an eye on him. Samatar was relieved when I told him. He said little, but I saw the flicker in his eyes, the look a son gives when he feels protected.

In those weeks, I talked to him more about his identity, who we were, and who his grandfather was. I told him stories of Baidoa, of Marka, of my journey from Somalia to Kenya, from Dadaab to Frankfurt and Helsinki, and eventually to this cold, wet island we now called home. I did not dress the stories up: I told him of the hardships, the hunger, the kindness of strangers, and the cruelty of others. I told him how, in all this, Allah was with us.

I wanted him to know that he was not adrift in the world, that he came from a people who had endured, prayed, and sacrificed, that he was Somali–not just by name, but by memory, by blood and by dignity. But I also wanted him to be British in the best way: to stand up for himself, to think freely, to be kind and just.

Sometimes we would walk together after *Maghrib*, just the two of us. He would talk about school, football, and sometimes girls, though shyly. I would just listen, but every now and then I would drop in a reminder, a verse from the Quran, or a Somali proverb. One night, as we passed the corner shop, he asked me, 'Aabo, do you miss your dad?'

I stopped walking. The question caught me unawares. I looked up at the sky, the stars hidden behind the city lights. 'Every day,' I said. 'But I'm grateful for the time we had. And I'm grateful that I get to be a Father to you.'

He said nothing, just nodded and kept walking, but he reached for my hand and held it for a moment. That moment is one I carry with me.

Hindiyeey has been my anchor through everything. Her strength humbles me. Even in her grief, she held our home together. Some mornings, I hear her making *dua* before *Fajr*, her voice low, asking for relief, for guidance for Samatar. Sometimes I think of all the women like her – displaced, tested, but unwavering – and I wonder whether they are the true pillars of our people.

We do not often talk of legacy in our culture. We speak of it in prayers, in names, in the hope that our children will remember us kindly, but these days I think about it more. What is the light we leave behind? Is it the titles we earn? The property we own? I think not; I believe it lies in how we have loved, how we have prayed, how we have guided those who come after us. I think it lies in the mercy we showed when we could have judged, in the words we offered when silence might have been easier.

I am not a perfect man; I have made many mistakes. But I try: I wake each day, and I try to be better than I was yesterday. I ask Allah for forgiveness. I ask Him to guide my son, to protect my wife, to have mercy on my parents.

And I hope – when my time comes, as it did for my Father – that those I leave behind will remember me not just for what I did, but for who I tried to be.

That, I believe, is the light we leave behind.

Epilogue: What Remains of Us

It had been four years since we returned from Garissa. My grief, though softened by time, had never truly left me. It settled into the quiet places of my days, like a shadow that stretches far but weighs nothing. My Father's absence was no longer a gaping wound but a presence, a memory that whispered more than it spoke. I often thought of his voice, his recitations of the Quran in the early mornings, his dry humour, and the way he carried silence with the wisdom of an elder. I remembered him most when I sat with the Quran open before me or when I prayed *Fajr* and lingered in *sujud*, asking Allah to have mercy on him and to forgive me my own shortcomings.

Samatar was now eighteen and preparing for university. He had grown taller than me, his shoulders broader, his walk more confident, but he still had the same quiet, observant gaze he had carried as a boy. Over the years, he had tested us in ways I had not expected. There had been two separate instances at school – nothing criminal or violent, but enough to shake us – a confrontation with a teacher over what he felt was unfair treatment, and a day's suspension for standing up for a younger Somali student who was being bullied. He was passionate, like I once had been and maybe still was.

I found myself often at the school, sitting opposite young white teachers who wanted to speak about policies and procedures while I wanted to talk about boys, guidance, and dignity. One told me that Samatar was 'too sensitive' and needed to 'toughen up'. I smiled, nodded, and told her, no, that what he needed was not to toughen up but to be understood, that sensitivity was not a flaw but, in our culture, a mark of deep humanity. After one meeting, I walked home alone, pausing at the *masjid*. I stayed longer than I needed, whispering my *dua* for Samatar – to be strong but gentle, proud but humble, Somali and British, without shame.

Hindiyeey was quieter now and more reflective. She still mentored from time to time – young girls came to her with their poems, their fears, their questions about God and growing up, but she no longer ran the youth programmes the way she once had. We walked more together, sometimes around the block, sometimes by the canal. She held my arm, not out of weakness, but habit; we had survived so much, she and I. Some mornings she would look at me and say, 'You're more your Father now.' I did not know what she meant at first, but I felt it too, in my stillness, my quiet worries, the way I answered slowly.

On Sundays, I would meet with three young men – one Somali, one Afghan, and one Jamaican – at the *masjid* library. They were not in trouble; they were simply lost, searching. There was no formal structure; we read a *hadith* or two; I told them stories about my boyhood in Baidoa, about my short time in Dadaab, about how I struggled in Europe when I arrived. They told me about their lives, what confused them, and how hard it was to be respectful when respect was not returned. I never judged them. I remembered what it felt like to be young and burning with questions.

My mother was still alive, although more frail. She lived with a relative in Nairobi. I spoke to her every Friday and, each time, she reminded me to make *dua*, to be patient, to forgive easily. 'Forgiveness,' she once told me, 'is what remains of us when strength is gone.' I wrote that down and kept it in my notebook.

Our house was calmer now. The laughter was quieter, the arguments fewer. Samatar sometimes played the Quran on his phone in the evenings while he was studying. He still listened to music, too, though more quietly when I was in the house. I watched him one night reading Surat Al-Kahf, his lips moving soundlessly. I stood at the door and did not interrupt. That moment stayed with me, not because it was extraordinary, but because it was ours.

I began writing again: nothing formal, just short essays, reflections about fatherhood, faith, and being caught between places. I called it 'Letters to My Father'. Sometimes I would read a passage aloud to Hindiyeey. She would listen, her eyes closed, and say, 'This one you must keep.'

There was a time when I feared dying suddenly, like my Father did. I fear that no longer. I feared leaving without light, without having passed on something that would remain. That is what I think about now – not success or titles, but what remains: a son who prays, a wife who remembers my words, a young man who stops himself in anger because he once heard me say, 'The Prophet never raised his voice unless it was for justice.'

As I sit now in the quiet room we call the study, although it is just a small corner of the house, I can hear the wind outside. The leaves are turning. Samatar is packing his books for university. Hindiyeey is humming softly in the kitchen. The call to *Maghrib* echoes from my phone. And I feel, for a moment, a stillness so complete it feels like mercy.

What remains of us is not always grand: it is the way we listen, the way we forgive, the way we remind someone to pray gently, not harshly. It lies in the stories we leave behind, the prayers whispered in secret, the way our grandchildren speak our names when we are gone.

And if that is all I leave, then I am at peace.

Glossary and Cultural Note for *My Name is Sahal*

Glossary of Non-English Words

Below is a comprehensive list of non-English words (primarily Somali and Arabic) used in the novel, with their meanings, approximate pronunciations (where relevant), and contextual usage to assist readers.

1. **Aabo**
   o **Language:** Somali
   o **Pronunciation:** AH-bo
   o **Meaning:** Father.
   o **Context:** Used by Sahal when addressing or referring to his father, Diinoow, in letters and dialogue (e.g., "Dear Aabo" in "Meeting Hindiyeey"). Reflects familial respect and affection in Somali culture.

2. **Abaayo**
   o **Language:** Somali
   o **Pronunciation:** Ah-BAH-yo
   o **Meaning:** Sister or a term of endearment for a close female relative or friend.
   o **Context:** Used by Hindiyeey's brother when addressing her (e.g., "Abaayo, we want to see you" in "Crossing into Hope") and by Samatar as his first word, referring to Hindiyeey's sister.

3. **Alhamdulillah**
   o **Language:** Arabic
   o **Pronunciation:** Al-HAM-du-lil-LAH
   o **Meaning:** Praise be to Allah.
   o **Context:** Frequently used by characters (e.g., Sahal's father in "The Birth of Samatar": "Alhamdulillah, Alhamdulillah") to express gratitude or relief, reflecting Islamic faith central to the characters' lives.

4. **Fajr**
   o **Language:** Arabic
   o **Pronunciation:** FAJ-er
   o **Meaning:** The dawn prayer, one of the five daily Islamic prayers.
   o **Context:** Mentioned in "The Day My Father Died" (e.g., "he never missed Fajr prayers") and "The Light We Leave Behind" to highlight characters' religious devotion.

5. **Gooni**
   o **Language:** Somali
   o **Pronunciation:** GO-nee
   o **Meaning:** Solitary one.
   o **Context:** Proposed as a name for Sahal by his mother in "A Boy With so Much Hair," based on local lore that children born on Wednesday are socially awkward.

6. **Haa**
   o **Language:** Somali
   o **Pronunciation:** HAH
   o **Meaning:** Yes.
   o **Context:** Used in dialogue, such as Sahal's response to his teacher ("Haa Macalin" in "From Ukuroow to Adan Dheere") and in conversations (e.g., "Haa

wali wuu ma qanyahay" in "Grief, Growth and Longing for a Father"), indicating agreement or affirmation.

7. **Halwa**
   o **Language:** Arabic/Somali
   o **Pronunciation:** HAL-wa
   o **Meaning:** A sweet confection, often made with sugar, ghee, and nuts, popular in Somali and Middle Eastern cultures.
   o **Context:** Aunt Dahaba brings halwa to Sahal's home (e.g., in "Grief, Growth and Longing for a Father"), symbolising hospitality and community.

8. **Himilo**
   o **Language:** Somali
   o **Pronunciation:** HEE-mi-lo
   o **Meaning:** Ambition or aspiration.
   o **Context:** Used as the name of the non-profit organisation, Himilo Mentorship Network, in "A House in the Trees," reflecting Sahal and Hindiyeey's mission to inspire Somali youth.

9. **Hooyo**
   o **Language:** Somali
   o **Pronunciation:** HO-yo
   o **Meaning:** Mother.
   o **Context:** Used by Sahal when addressing his mother, Suleey (e.g., "Haye, Hooyo" in "From Ukuroow to Adan Dheere"), and by his mother when addressing him affectionately (e.g., "Sahal, wake up, Hooyo!" in the same section).

10. **Istikhara**
    o **Language:** Arabic
    o **Pronunciation:** Is-tik-HA-ra

o **Meaning:** A prayer for guidance in making decisions, performed by Muslims.
o **Context:** Mentioned in "Crossing into Hope" ("We said an Istikhara prayer that night") when Sahal and Hindiyeey decide to move to the UK, emphasising reliance on divine guidance.

11. **Istighfar**
   o **Language:** Arabic
   o **Pronunciation:** Is-tig-FAR
   o **Meaning:** Seeking forgiveness from Allah.
   o **Context:** Used in "The Light We Leave Behind" ("making istighfar, seeking forgiveness") to show Sahal's spiritual reflection after his father's death.

12. **Kuuloow**
   o **Language:** Somali
   o **Pronunciation:** KOO-low
   o **Meaning:** Darkie, referring to a dark complexion.
   o **Context:** Proposed as a name for Sahal by Sonkoreey in "A Boy With so Much Hair" due to his darker complexion, but rejected.

13. **Macalin**
   o **Language:** Somali
   o **Pronunciation:** Ma-KA-lin
   o **Meaning:** Teacher.
   o **Context:** Used to address teachers, such as Macalin Adan Dheere (e.g., "Haa Macalin" in "From Ukuroow to Adan Dheere") and Saneey, reflecting respect for educators in Somali culture.

14. **Maay-Maay**
   o **Language:** Somali
   o **Pronunciation:** MY-MY

o **Meaning:** A dialect of the Somali language spoken primarily in southern Somalia, including Baidoa.

o **Context:** Frequently referenced (e.g., in "A Boy With so Much Hair" and "Grief, Growth and Longing for a Father") to denote the dialect spoken by Sahal's mother and grandmother, distinguishing regional identity.

15. **Af-Mahaa-tiri**

o **Language:** Somali

o **Pronunciation:** Af-Ma-HAA-tee-ree

o **Meaning:** A dialect of the Somali language, also known as Maxaa Tiri, spoken in northern and central Somalia.

o **Context:** Used in "Grief, Growth and Longing for a Father" to describe the dialect of the man delivering Diinoow's letter, highlighting linguistic diversity in Somalia.

16. **Rak'ah**

o **Language:** Arabic

o **Pronunciation:** RAH-kah

o **Meaning:** A unit of prayer in Islam, consisting of a sequence of standing, bowing, and prostrating.

o **Context:** Mentioned in "The Day My Father Died" ("I prayed two rakah") to describe Sahal's prayer for his father's soul.

17. **Rooboow**

o **Language:** Somali

o **Pronunciation:** ROO-bow

o **Meaning:** Rainy season.

o **Context:** Proposed as a name for Sahal by his grandmother Nuurto in "A Boy With so Much Hair," reflecting the season of his birth.

18. **Sahal**
    - o **Language:** Somali
    - o **Pronunciation:** SA-hal
    - o **Meaning:** Easy or effortless.
    - o **Context:** Chosen as Sahal's name in "A Boy With so Much Hair" due to his easy birth, symbolising simplicity and resilience throughout his journey.

19. **Sujud**
    - o **Language:** Arabic
    - o **Pronunciation:** Soo-JOOD
    - o **Meaning:** Prostration, the act of bowing down in Islamic prayer.
    - o **Context:** Used in "The Day My Father Died" ("I lingered in sujud") to describe Sahal's prayer posture, emphasising spiritual humility.

Cultural Note for Non-Somali Readers

My Name is Sahal is deeply rooted in Somali culture, Islamic faith, and the experiences of displacement and diaspora. Below is a cultural note to help non-Somali readers understand key aspects of the novel's context and significance.

Somali Culture and Traditions

- **Nomadic Heritage:** The novel begins in rural Somalia, where Sahal's early years are shaped by a nomadic lifestyle (e.g., living among goats and sheep in "A Boy With so Much Hair"). Somalia has a strong nomadic tradition, with many families historically relying on livestock herding. The incident with the stampeding camel underscores the challenges and dangers of this lifestyle, prompting the move to Baidoa for safety and education.
- **Naming Ceremonies:** The naming of Sahal in "A Boy With so Much Hair" reflects Somali traditions where

family members gather to propose names, often based on circumstances of birth, physical traits, or cultural beliefs (e.g., "Gooni" for a Wednesday-born child). Names carry significant meaning and are chosen to reflect hopes or characteristics for the child.

- **Family and Community**: Somali culture emphasises strong family and community ties. Extended family members, like Aunt Dahaba and Great-Aunt Sonkoreey, play crucial roles in supporting Sahal and his mother. The communal response to grief (e.g., condolences after Nuurto's and Diinoow's deaths) reflects the collective nature of Somali mourning practices.

- **Language and Dialects**: Somalia is linguistically diverse, with dialects like Maay-Maay (spoken in southern regions like Baidoa) and Af-Mahaa-tiri (Maxaa Tiri, more widely spoken). The novel uses these dialects to highlight regional identities and social interactions (e.g., the letter delivery in "Grief, Growth and Longing for a Father"). Somali is the primary language, but Italian influence (e.g., Aunt Dahaba's fluency) reflects Somalia's colonial history under Italy.

Islamic Faith

- **Religious Practices**: Islam is central to the characters' lives, shaping their responses to joy, grief, and decision-making. Terms like "Alhamdulillah," "Fajr," "Istikhara," "sujud," and "rak'ah" reflect daily practices such as prayer, seeking forgiveness, and guidance. These practices provide spiritual grounding for Sahal, especially during crises (e.g., praying after his father's death in "The Day My Father Died").

- **Community and Mosques**: Mosques are not just places of worship but also community hubs, as seen in "Crossing into Hope" (Sahal meeting Yusuf at the mosque) and "The Light We Leave Behind" (mentoring youth at the masjid library). They represent spaces of connection and support for the Somali diaspora.

Displacement and Diaspora

- **Civil War and Migration:** The novel references the Somali Civil War (implicitly in the prologue's mention of war tearing through Mogadishu), which forced Sahal and his family to flee to Kenya, then Europe. This reflects the broader Somali diaspora experience, with millions displaced since the 1990s due to conflict, seeking refuge in camps like Dadaab or cities like Frankfurt, Helsinki, and Manchester.
- **Asylum and Integration:** Sahal's struggles with asylum rejections (e.g., in Germany and Finland) and eventual success in the UK highlight the challenges of navigating immigration systems. The Somali community in Manchester, with its halal butchers and cafés, illustrates the diaspora's efforts to recreate cultural spaces abroad, as seen in "Starting Over in Manchester."
- **Education as Empowerment:** Education is a recurring theme, from Sahal's early schooling in Baidoa to his degree in Manchester. For many Somalis, education is a pathway to stability and dignity in the diaspora, as reflected in Sahal's journey and the establishment of Himilo Mentorship Network.

Historical and Geographical Context

- **Baidoa and Mogadishu:** Baidoa, described as a lush, urban centre in the novel, is a significant city in southern Somalia, known for its agricultural region but also affected by conflict and famine. Mogadishu, mentioned as the site of war, is Somalia's capital and a historical hub of trade and culture.

- **Marka and Garissa:** Marka, where Sahal attends boarding school, is a coastal city in Somalia, while Garissa, where his parents later reside, is a Kenyan town with a large Somali population, often a destination for refugees.
- **Manchester's Somali Community:** Manchester hosts one of the UK's largest Somali communities, concentrated in areas like Moss Side and Longsight. The novel's depiction of community centres, mosques, and Somali businesses reflects this vibrant diaspora, which supports new arrivals through networks like the one Sahal and Hindiyeey build.

Notes for Readers

- **Emotional Resonance:** The novel's themes of loss, love, and resilience are universal, but they are deeply tied to Somali experiences of displacement and faith. Non-Somali readers may find the frequent references to prayer and family dynamics unfamiliar but should see them as expressions of cultural identity and survival.
- **Cultural Sensitivity:** Terms like "Kuuloow" (darkie) reflect cultural naming practices based on physical traits, not derogatory intent in the Somali context. Similarly, the strong emphasis on family honour and community support may differ from Western individualism but is central to the characters' motivations.
- **Historical Nuance:** The novel spans the 1970s to the 2020s, covering Somalia's pre-war optimism, the civil war's devastation, and the diaspora's challenges. Readers unfamiliar with this history may benefit from noting that Somalia's collapse in the 1990s led to widespread migration, shaping Sahal's journey.

About the Author

 **Dr. Nuur Hassan** is a UK-based author whose work explores themes of exile, identity, faith, and belonging. *My Name is Sahal*, his third book and first novel, marks his debut into literary fiction after two earlier works of non-fiction.

Known for his reflective and poetic style, Dr. Hassan's writing draws on the silences, displacements, and spiritual depth of the Somali diaspora experience. Through essays, books, and storytelling, he weaves narratives that bridge continents and generations, capturing both the struggles and the resilience of migrant lives.

With *My Name is Sahal*, he invites readers into a world shaped by memory and faith, where the search for home becomes a journey of the heart as much as of geography.